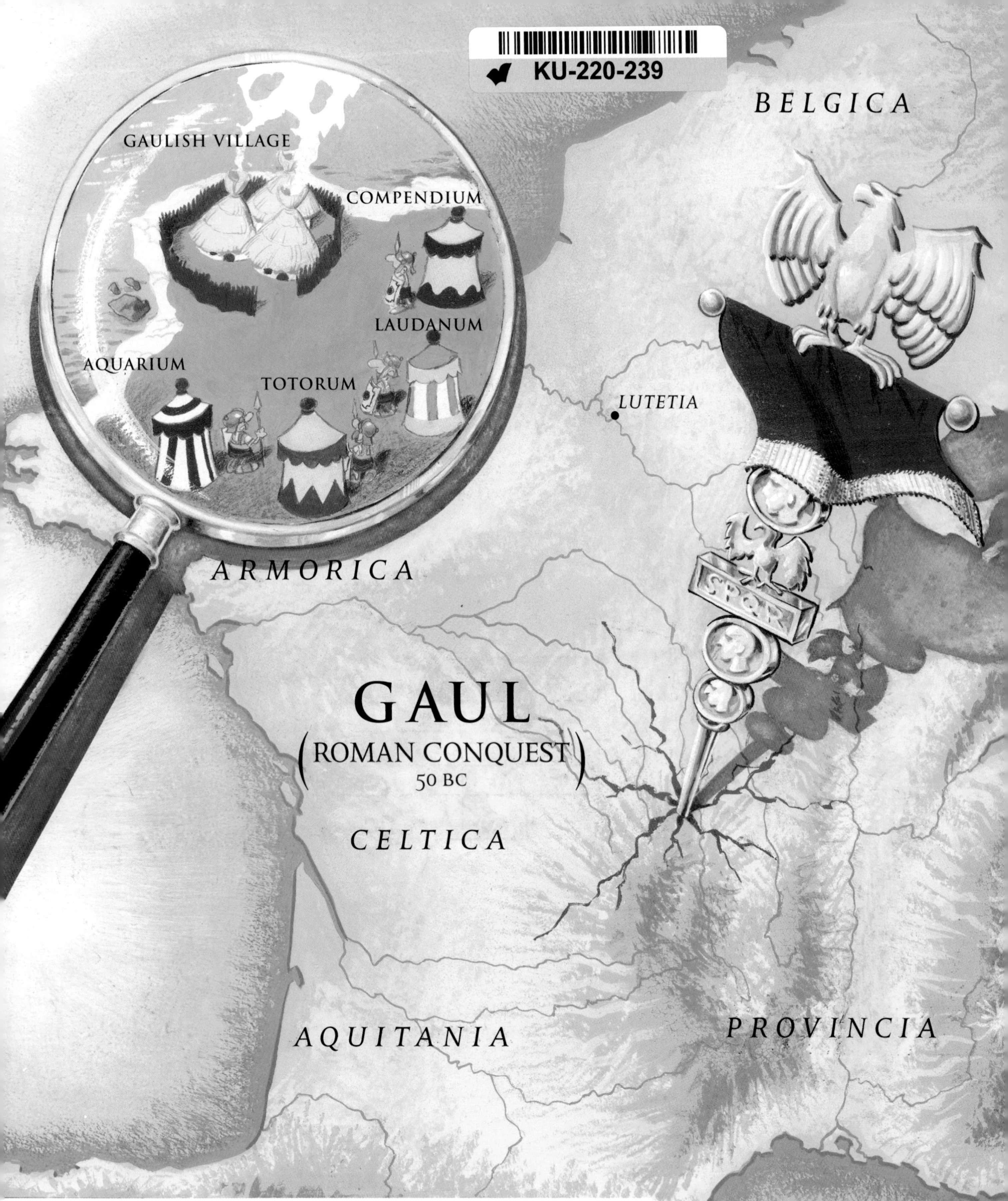
GAULISH VILLAGE
COMPENDIUM
LAUDANUM
AQUARIUM
TOTORUM
BELGICA
LUTETIA
SPQR
ARMORICA
GAUL
(ROMAN CONQUEST)
50 BC
CELTICA
AQUITANIA
PROVINCIA

THE YEAR IS 50 BC. GAUL IS ENTIRELY OCCUPIED BY THE ROMANS. WELL, NOT ENTIRELY . . . ONE SMALL VILLAGE OF THE INDOMITABLE GAULS STILL HOLDS OUT AGAINST THE INVADERS. AND LIFE IS NOT EASY FOR THE ROMAN LEGIONARIES WHO GARRISON THE FORTIFIED CAMPS OF TOTORUM, AQUARIUM, LAUDANUM AND COMPENDIUM . . .

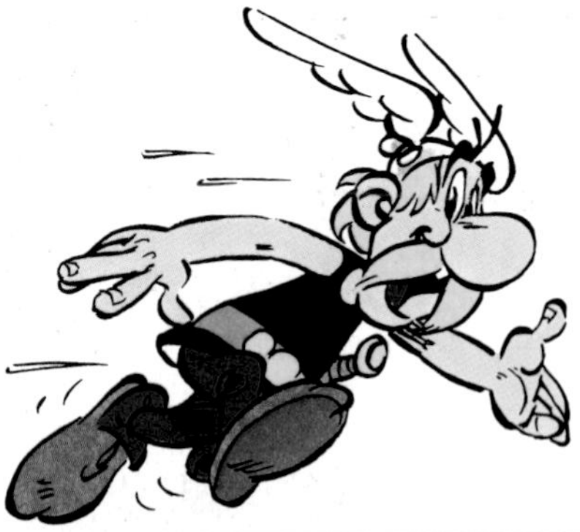

ASTERIX, THE HERO OF THESE ADVENTURES. A SHREWD, CUNNING LITTLE WARRIOR, ALL PERILOUS MISSIONS ARE IMMEDIATELY ENTRUSTED TO HIM. ASTERIX GETS HIS SUPERHUMAN STRENGTH FROM THE MAGIC POTION BREWED BY THE DRUID GETAFIX . . .

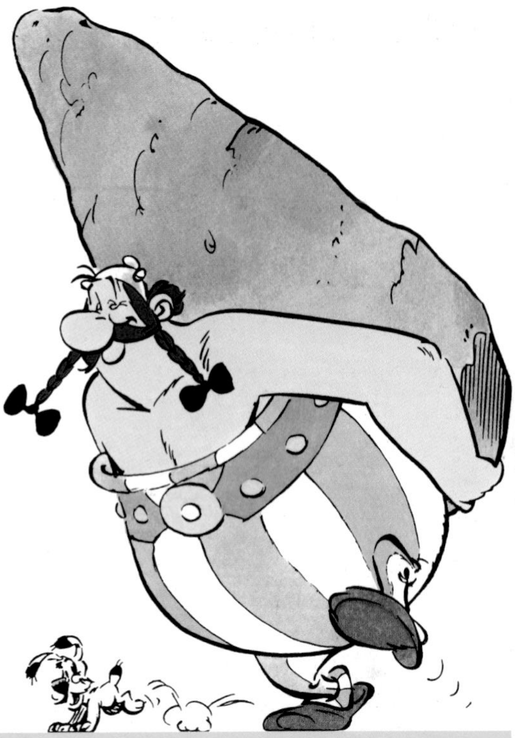

OBELIX, ASTERIX'S INSEPARABLE FRIEND. A MENHIR DELIVERY-MAN BY TRADE, ADDICTED TO WILD BOAR. OBELIX IS ALWAYS READY TO DROP EVERYTHING AND GO OFF ON A NEW ADVENTURE WITH ASTERIX – SO LONG AS THERE'S WILD BOAR TO EAT, AND PLENTY OF FIGHTING. HIS CONSTANT COMPANION IS DOGMATIX, THE ONLY KNOWN CANINE ECOLOGIST, WHO HOWLS WITH DESPAIR WHEN A TREE IS CUT DOWN.

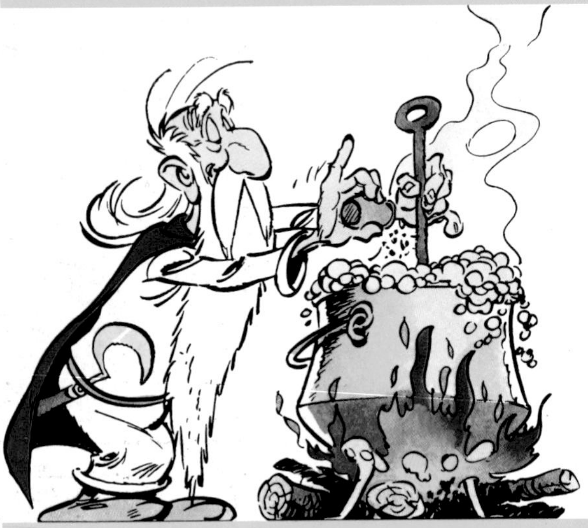

GETAFIX, THE VENERABLE VILLAGE DRUID, GATHERS MISTLETOE AND BREWS MAGIC POTIONS. HIS SPECIALITY IS THE POTION WHICH GIVES THE DRINKER SUPERHUMAN STRENGTH. BUT GETAFIX ALSO HAS OTHER RECIPES UP HIS SLEEVE . . .

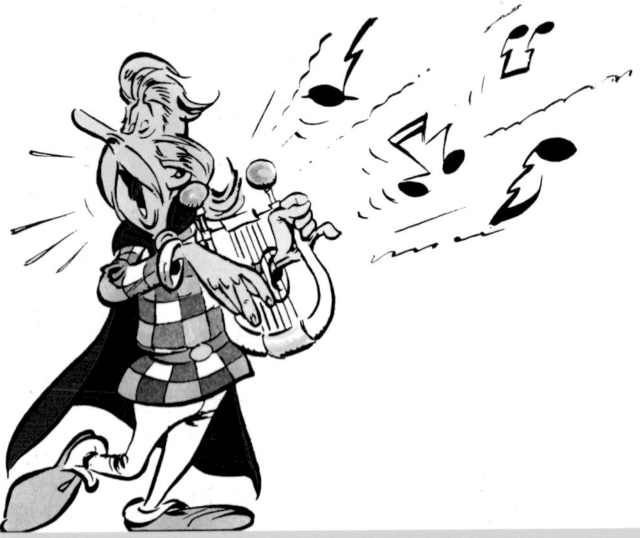

CACOFONIX, THE BARD. OPINION IS DIVIDED AS TO HIS MUSICAL GIFTS. CACOFONIX THINKS HE'S A GENIUS. EVERYONE ELSE THINKS HE'S UNSPEAKABLE. BUT SO LONG AS HE DOESN'T SPEAK, LET ALONE SING, EVERYBODY LIKES HIM . . .

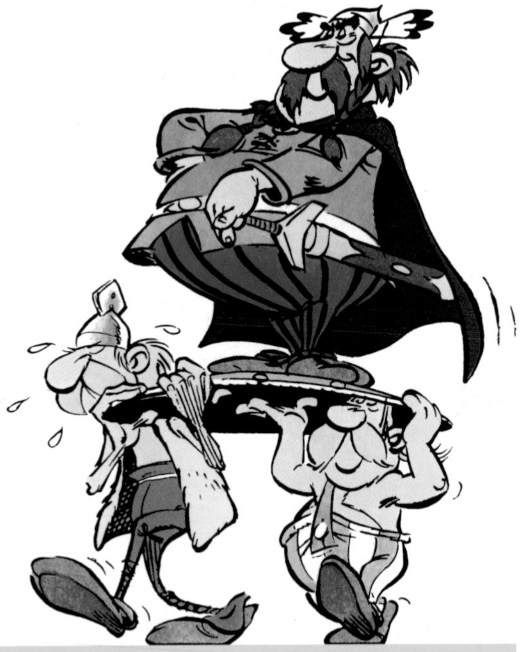

FINALLY, VITALSTATISTIX, THE CHIEF OF THE TRIBE. MAJESTIC, BRAVE AND HOT-TEMPERED, THE OLD WARRIOR IS RESPECTED BY HIS MEN AND FEARED BY HIS ENEMIES. VITALSTATISTIX HIMSELF HAS ONLY ONE FEAR, HE IS AFRAID THE SKY MAY FALL ON HIS HEAD TOMORROW. BUT AS HE ALWAYS SAYS, TOMORROW NEVER COMES.

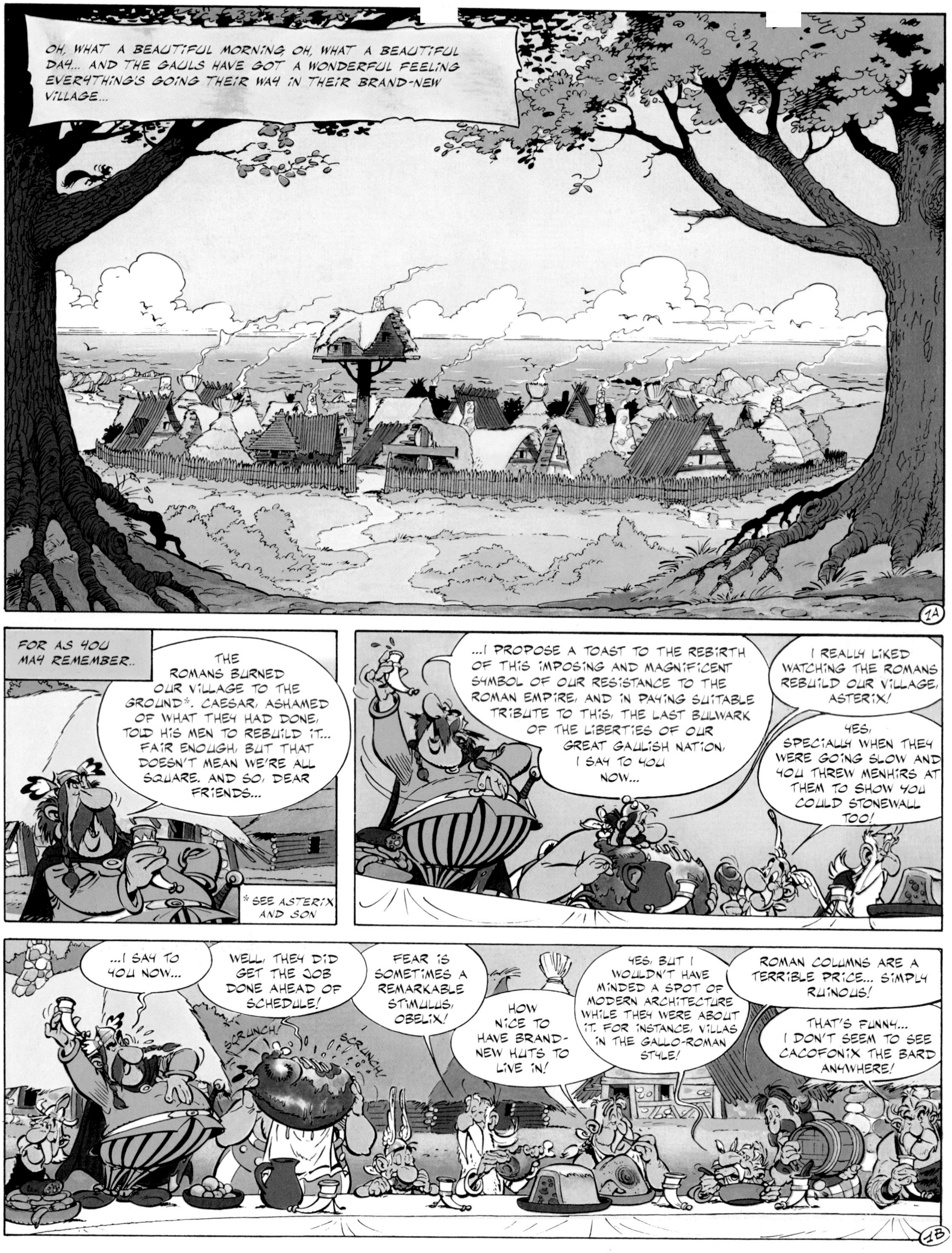
OH, WHAT A BEAUTIFUL MORNING, OH, WHAT A BEAUTIFUL DAY... AND THE GAULS HAVE GOT A WONDERFUL FEELING EVERYTHING'S GOING THEIR WAY IN THEIR BRAND-NEW VILLAGE...
FOR AS YOU MAY REMEMBER..
THE ROMANS BURNED OUR VILLAGE TO THE GROUND*. CAESAR, ASHAMED OF WHAT THEY HAD DONE, TOLD HIS MEN TO REBUILD IT... FAIR ENOUGH, BUT THAT DOESN'T MEAN WE'RE ALL SQUARE. AND SO, DEAR FRIENDS...
* SEE ASTERIX AND SON
...I PROPOSE A TOAST TO THE REBIRTH OF THIS IMPOSING AND MAGNIFICENT SYMBOL OF OUR RESISTANCE TO THE ROMAN EMPIRE, AND IN PAYING SUITABLE TRIBUTE TO THIS, THE LAST BULWARK OF THE LIBERTIES OF OUR GREAT GAULISH NATION, I SAY TO YOU NOW...
I REALLY LIKED WATCHING THE ROMANS REBUILD OUR VILLAGE, ASTERIX!
YES, SPECIALLY WHEN THEY WERE GOING SLOW AND YOU THREW MENHIRS AT THEM TO SHOW YOU COULD STONEWALL TOO!
...I SAY TO YOU NOW...
SCRUNCH!
SCRUNCH!
WELL, THEY DID GET THE JOB DONE AHEAD OF SCHEDULE!
FEAR IS SOMETIMES A REMARKABLE STIMULUS, OBELIX!
HOW NICE TO HAVE BRAND-NEW HUTS TO LIVE IN!
YES, BUT I WOULDN'T HAVE MINDED A SPOT OF MODERN ARCHITECTURE WHILE THEY WERE ABOUT IT. FOR INSTANCE, VILLAS IN THE GALLO-ROMAN STYLE!
ROMAN COLUMNS ARE A TERRIBLE PRICE... SIMPLY RUINOUS!
THAT'S FUNNY... I DON'T SEEM TO SEE CACOFONIX THE BARD ANYWHERE!
1A
1B

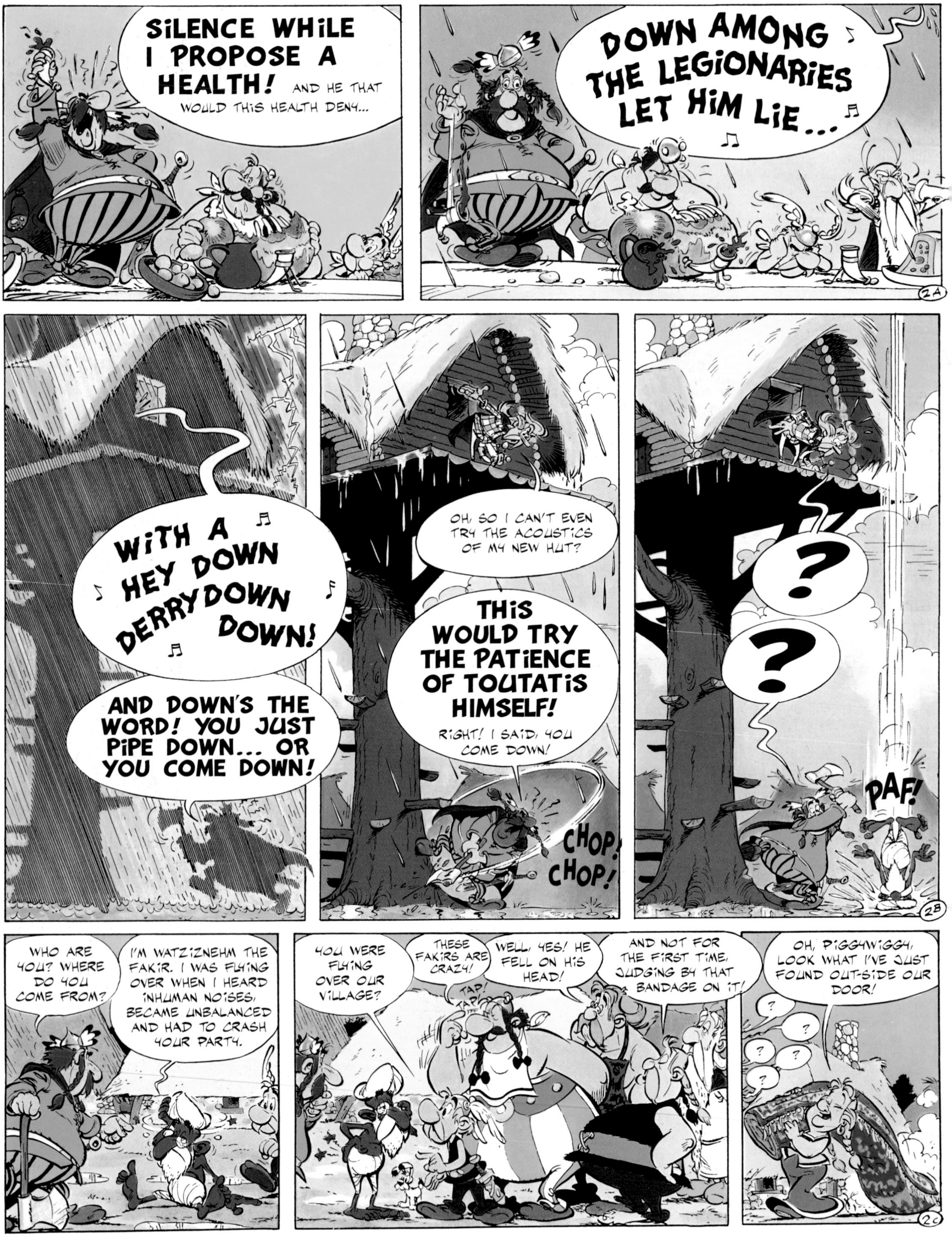
SILENCE WHILE I PROPOSE A HEALTH!
AND HE THAT WOULD THIS HEALTH DENY...
DOWN AMONG THE LEGIONARIES LET HIM LIE...
2A
WITH A HEY DOWN DERRYDOWN DOWN!
AND DOWN'S THE WORD! YOU JUST PIPE DOWN... OR YOU COME DOWN!
OH, SO I CAN'T EVEN TRY THE ACOUSTICS OF MY NEW HUT?
THIS WOULD TRY THE PATIENCE OF TOUTATIS HIMSELF!
RIGHT! I SAID, YOU COME DOWN!
CHOP! CHOP!
?
?
PAF!
2B
WHO ARE YOU? WHERE DO YOU COME FROM?
I'M WATZIZNEHM THE FAKIR. I WAS FLYING OVER WHEN I HEARD INHUMAN NOISES, BECAME UNBALANCED AND HAD TO CRASH YOUR PARTY.
YOU WERE FLYING OVER OUR VILLAGE?
THESE FAKIRS ARE CRAZY!
TAP! TAP!
WELL, YES! HE FELL ON HIS HEAD!
AND NOT FOR THE FIRST TIME, JUDGING BY THAT BANDAGE ON IT!
OH, PIGGYWIGGY, LOOK WHAT I'VE JUST FOUND OUT-SIDE OUR DOOR!
?
?
?
?
?
2C

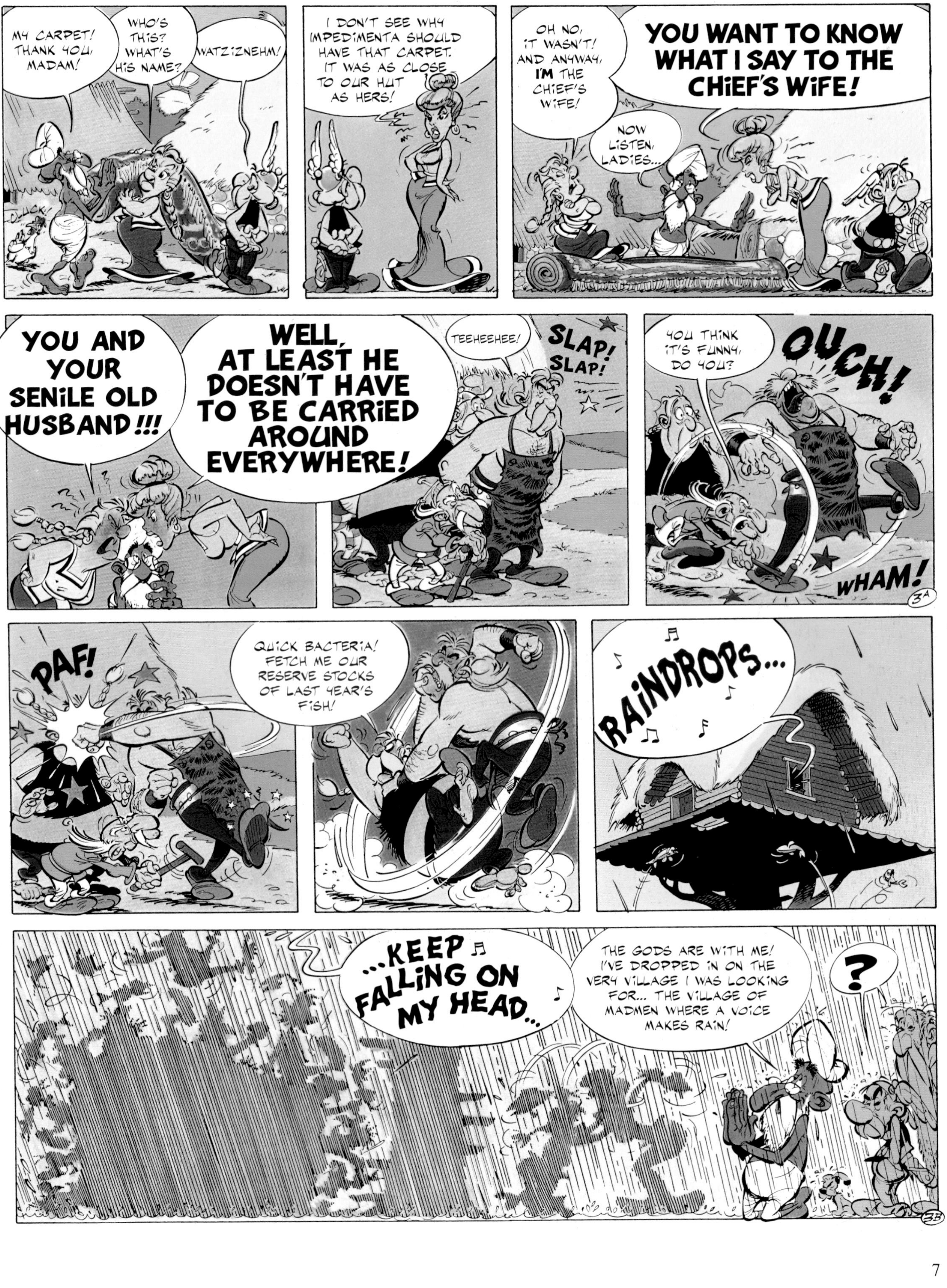

MY CARPET! THANK YOU, MADAM!
WHO'S THIS? WHAT'S HIS NAME?
WATZIZNEHM!
CLUCK!
I DON'T SEE WHY IMPEDIMENTA SHOULD HAVE THAT CARPET. IT WAS AS CLOSE TO OUR HUT AS HERS!
OH NO, IT WASN'T! AND ANYWAY, I'M THE CHIEF'S WIFE!
YOU WANT TO KNOW WHAT I SAY TO THE CHIEF'S WIFE!
NOW LISTEN, LADIES...
YOU AND YOUR SENILE OLD HUSBAND!!!
WELL, AT LEAST HE DOESN'T HAVE TO BE CARRIED AROUND EVERYWHERE!
TEEHEEHEE!
SLAP! SLAP!
YOU THINK IT'S FUNNY, DO YOU?
OUCH!
WHAM!
3A
PAF!
QUICK BACTERIA! FETCH ME OUR RESERVE STOCKS OF LAST YEAR'S FISH!
RAINDROPS...
...KEEP FALLING ON MY HEAD...
THE GODS ARE WITH ME! I'VE DROPPED IN ON THE VERY VILLAGE I WAS LOOKING FOR... THE VILLAGE OF MADMEN WHERE A VOICE MAKES RAIN!
?
3B

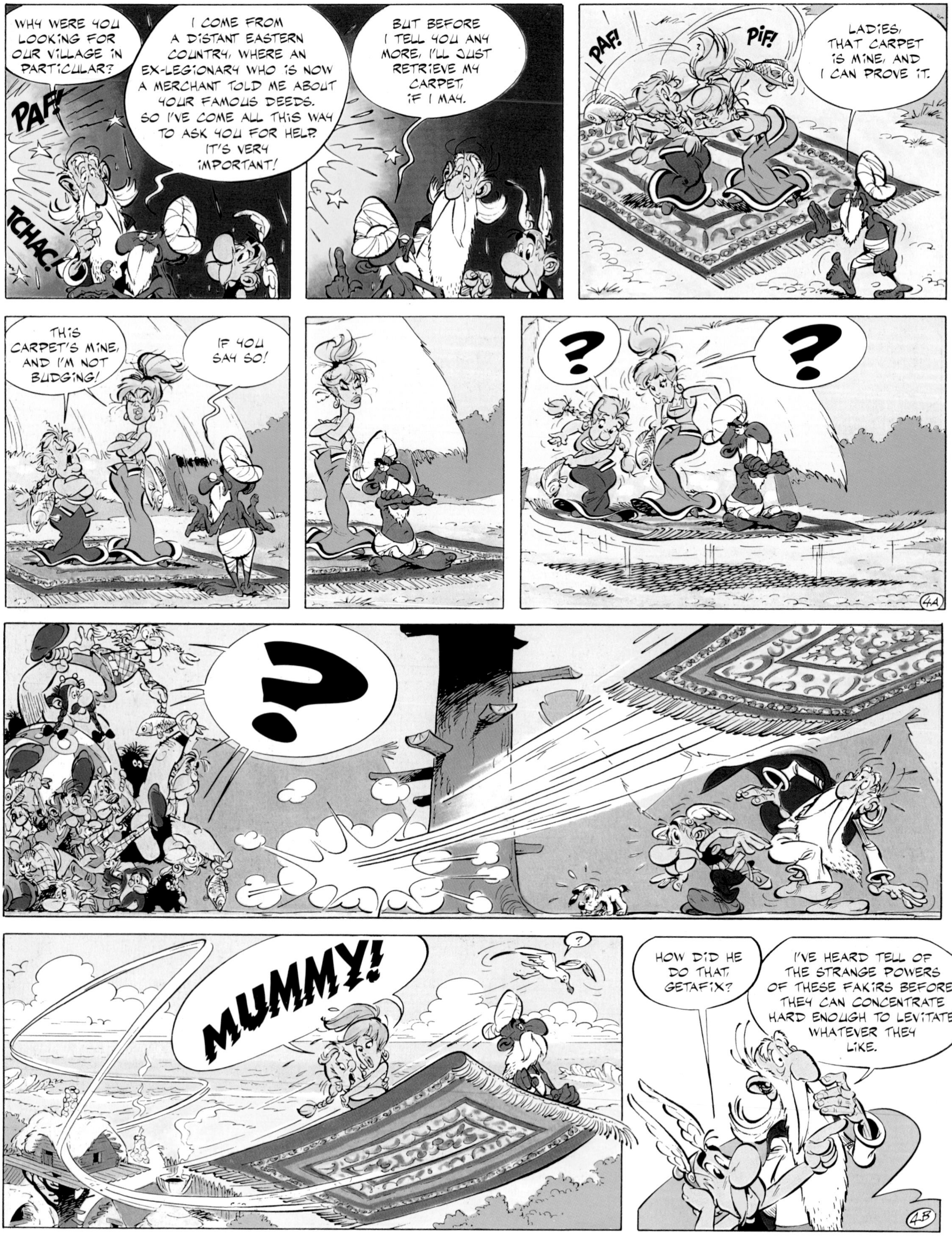
WHY WERE YOU LOOKING FOR OUR VILLAGE IN PARTICULAR?
PAF!
TCHAC!
I COME FROM A DISTANT EASTERN COUNTRY, WHERE AN EX-LEGIONARY WHO IS NOW A MERCHANT TOLD ME ABOUT YOUR FAMOUS DEEDS. SO I'VE COME ALL THIS WAY TO ASK YOU FOR HELP. IT'S VERY IMPORTANT!
BUT BEFORE I TELL YOU ANY MORE, I'LL JUST RETRIEVE MY CARPET, IF I MAY.
PAF!
PIF!
LADIES, THAT CARPET IS MINE, AND I CAN PROVE IT.
THIS CARPET'S MINE, AND I'M NOT BUDGING!
IF YOU SAY SO!
?
?
?
MUMMY!
?
HOW DID HE DO THAT, GETAFIX?
I'VE HEARD TELL OF THE STRANGE POWERS OF THESE FAKIRS BEFORE. THEY CAN CONCENTRATE HARD ENOUGH TO LEVITATE WHATEVER THEY LIKE.

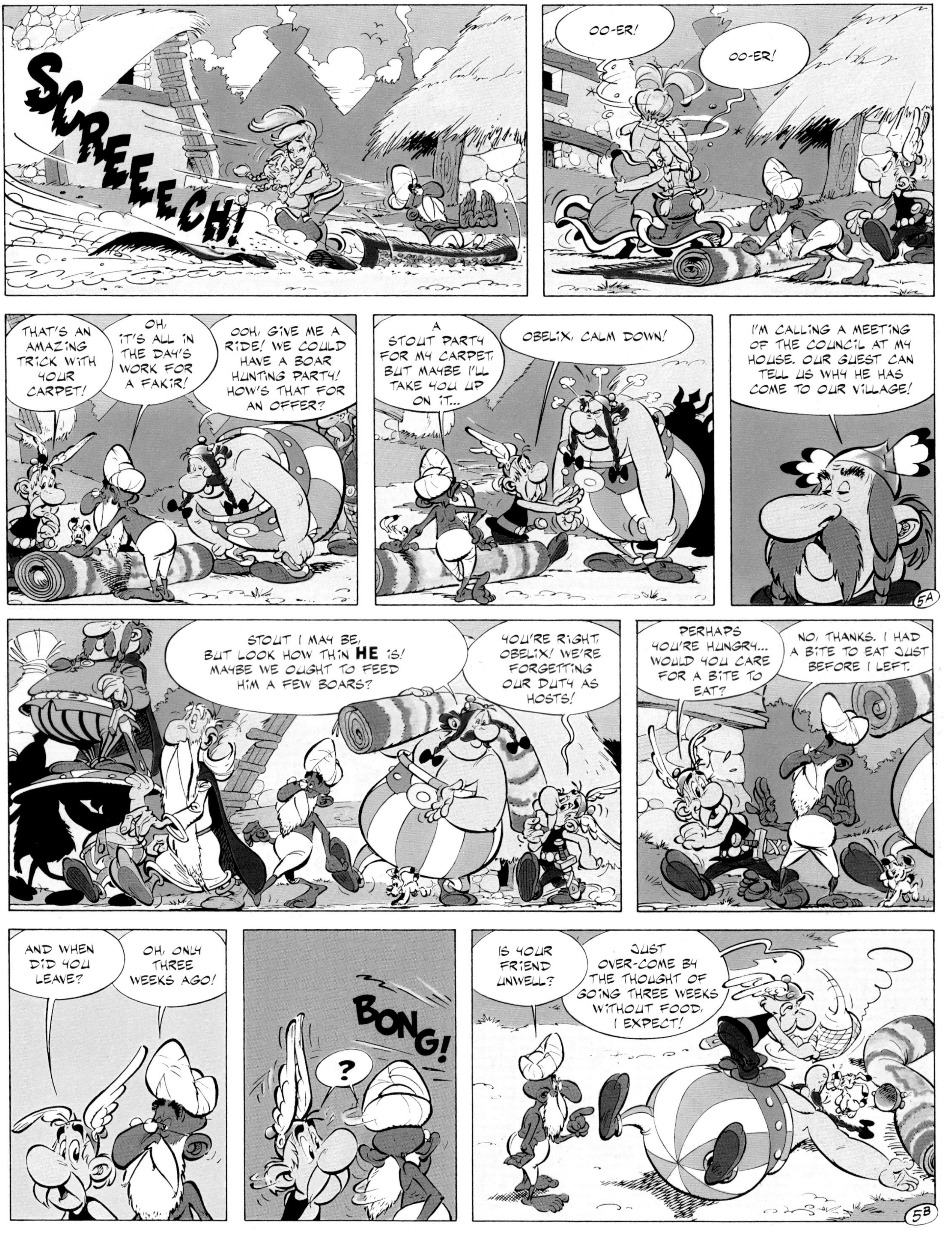
SCREEEECH!
OO-ER!
OO-ER!
THAT'S AN AMAZING TRICK WITH YOUR CARPET!
OH, IT'S ALL IN THE DAY'S WORK FOR A FAKIR!
OOH, GIVE ME A RIDE! WE COULD HAVE A BOAR HUNTING PARTY! HOW'S THAT FOR AN OFFER?
A STOUT PARTY FOR MY CARPET, BUT MAYBE I'LL TAKE YOU UP ON IT...
OBELIX, CALM DOWN!
I'M CALLING A MEETING OF THE COUNCIL AT MY HOUSE. OUR GUEST CAN TELL US WHY HE HAS COME TO OUR VILLAGE!
5A
STOUT I MAY BE, BUT LOOK HOW THIN HE IS! MAYBE WE OUGHT TO FEED HIM A FEW BOARS?
YOU'RE RIGHT, OBELIX! WE'RE FORGETTING OUR DUTY AS HOSTS!
PERHAPS YOU'RE HUNGRY... WOULD YOU CARE FOR A BITE TO EAT?
NO, THANKS. I HAD A BITE TO EAT JUST BEFORE I LEFT.
AND WHEN DID YOU LEAVE?
OH, ONLY THREE WEEKS AGO!
BONG!
?
IS YOUR FRIEND UNWELL?
JUST OVER-COME BY THE THOUGHT OF GOING THREE WEEKS WITHOUT FOOD, I EXPECT!
5B

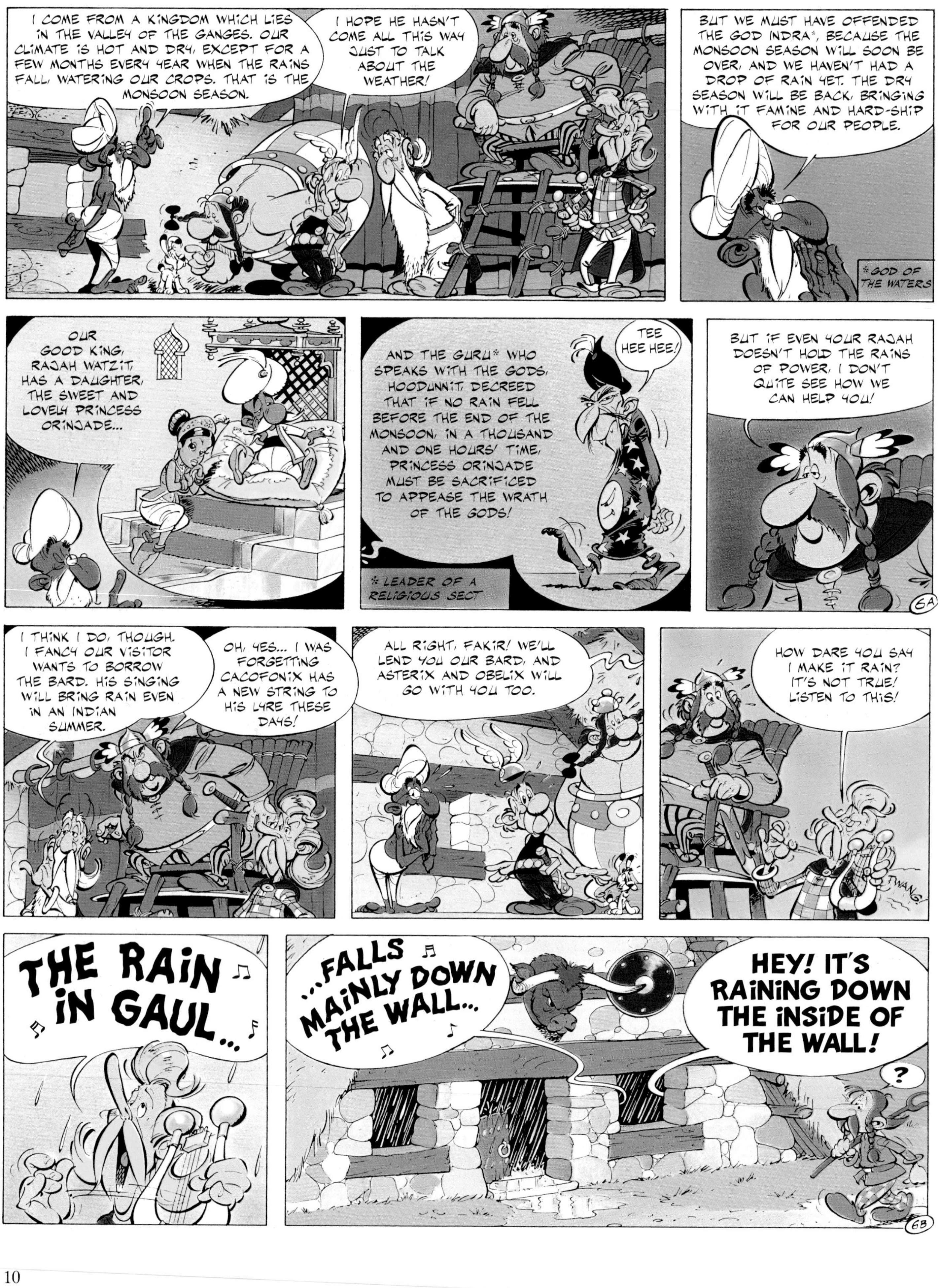
I COME FROM A KINGDOM WHICH LIES IN THE VALLEY OF THE GANGES. OUR CLIMATE IS HOT AND DRY, EXCEPT FOR A FEW MONTHS EVERY YEAR WHEN THE RAINS FALL, WATERING OUR CROPS. THAT IS THE MONSOON SEASON.
I HOPE HE HASN'T COME ALL THIS WAY JUST TO TALK ABOUT THE WEATHER!
BUT WE MUST HAVE OFFENDED THE GOD INDRA*, BECAUSE THE MONSOON SEASON WILL SOON BE OVER, AND WE HAVEN'T HAD A DROP OF RAIN YET. THE DRY SEASON WILL BE BACK, BRINGING WITH IT FAMINE AND HARD-SHIP FOR OUR PEOPLE.
* GOD OF THE WATERS
OUR GOOD KING, RAJAH WATZIT, HAS A DAUGHTER, THE SWEET AND LOVELY PRINCESS ORINJADE...
AND THE GURU* WHO SPEAKS WITH THE GODS, HOODUNNIT, DECREED THAT IF NO RAIN FELL BEFORE THE END OF THE MONSOON, IN A THOUSAND AND ONE HOURS' TIME, PRINCESS ORINJADE MUST BE SACRIFICED TO APPEASE THE WRATH OF THE GODS!
TEE HEE HEE!
* LEADER OF A RELIGIOUS SECT
BUT IF EVEN YOUR RAJAH DOESN'T HOLD THE RAINS OF POWER, I DON'T QUITE SEE HOW WE CAN HELP YOU!
6A
I THINK I DO, THOUGH. I FANCY OUR VISITOR WANTS TO BORROW THE BARD. HIS SINGING WILL BRING RAIN EVEN IN AN INDIAN SUMMER.
OH, YES... I WAS FORGETTING CACOFONIX HAS A NEW STRING TO HIS LYRE THESE DAYS!
ALL RIGHT, FAKIR! WE'LL LEND YOU OUR BARD, AND ASTERIX AND OBELIX WILL GO WITH YOU TOO.
HOW DARE YOU SAY I MAKE IT RAIN? IT'S NOT TRUE! LISTEN TO THIS!
TWANG!
THE RAIN IN GAUL...
...FALLS MAINLY DOWN THE WALL...
HEY! IT'S RAINING DOWN THE INSIDE OF THE WALL!
?
6B

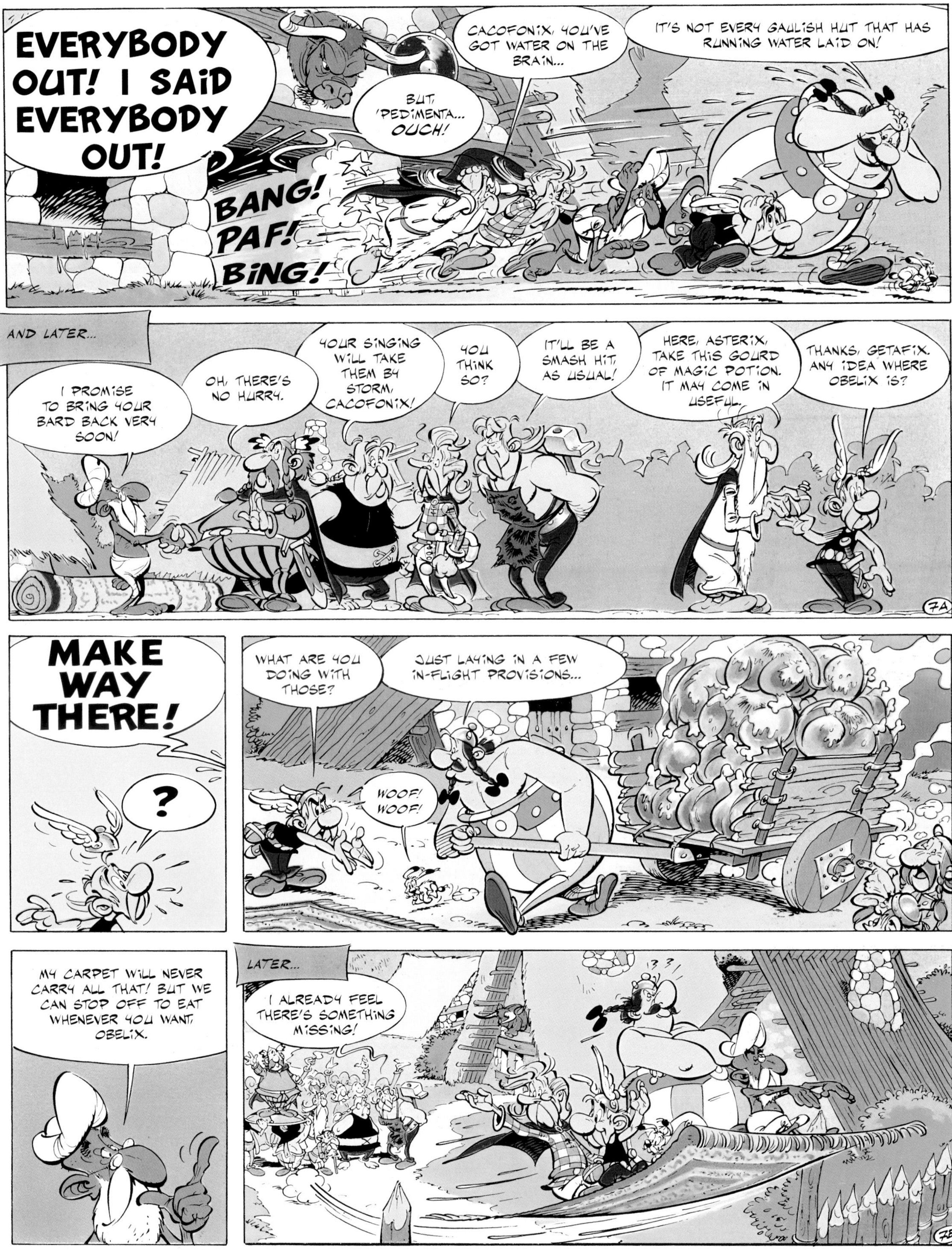
EVERYBODY OUT! I SAID EVERYBODY OUT!
BUT, 'PEDIMENTA... OUCH!
CACOFONIX, YOU'VE GOT WATER ON THE BRAIN...
IT'S NOT EVERY GAULISH HUT THAT HAS RUNNING WATER LAID ON!
BANG! PAF! BING!
AND LATER...
I PROMISE TO BRING YOUR BARD BACK VERY SOON!
OH, THERE'S NO HURRY.
YOUR SINGING WILL TAKE THEM BY STORM, CACOFONIX!
YOU THINK SO?
IT'LL BE A SMASH HIT, AS USUAL!
HERE, ASTERIX, TAKE THIS GOURD OF MAGIC POTION. IT MAY COME IN USEFUL.
THANKS, GETAFIX. ANY IDEA WHERE OBELIX IS?
7A
MAKE WAY THERE!
?
WHAT ARE YOU DOING WITH THOSE?
JUST LAYING IN A FEW IN-FLIGHT PROVISIONS...
WOOF! WOOF!
MY CARPET WILL NEVER CARRY ALL THAT! BUT WE CAN STOP OFF TO EAT WHENEVER YOU WANT, OBELIX.
LATER...
I ALREADY FEEL THERE'S SOMETHING MISSING!
? ? ?
7B

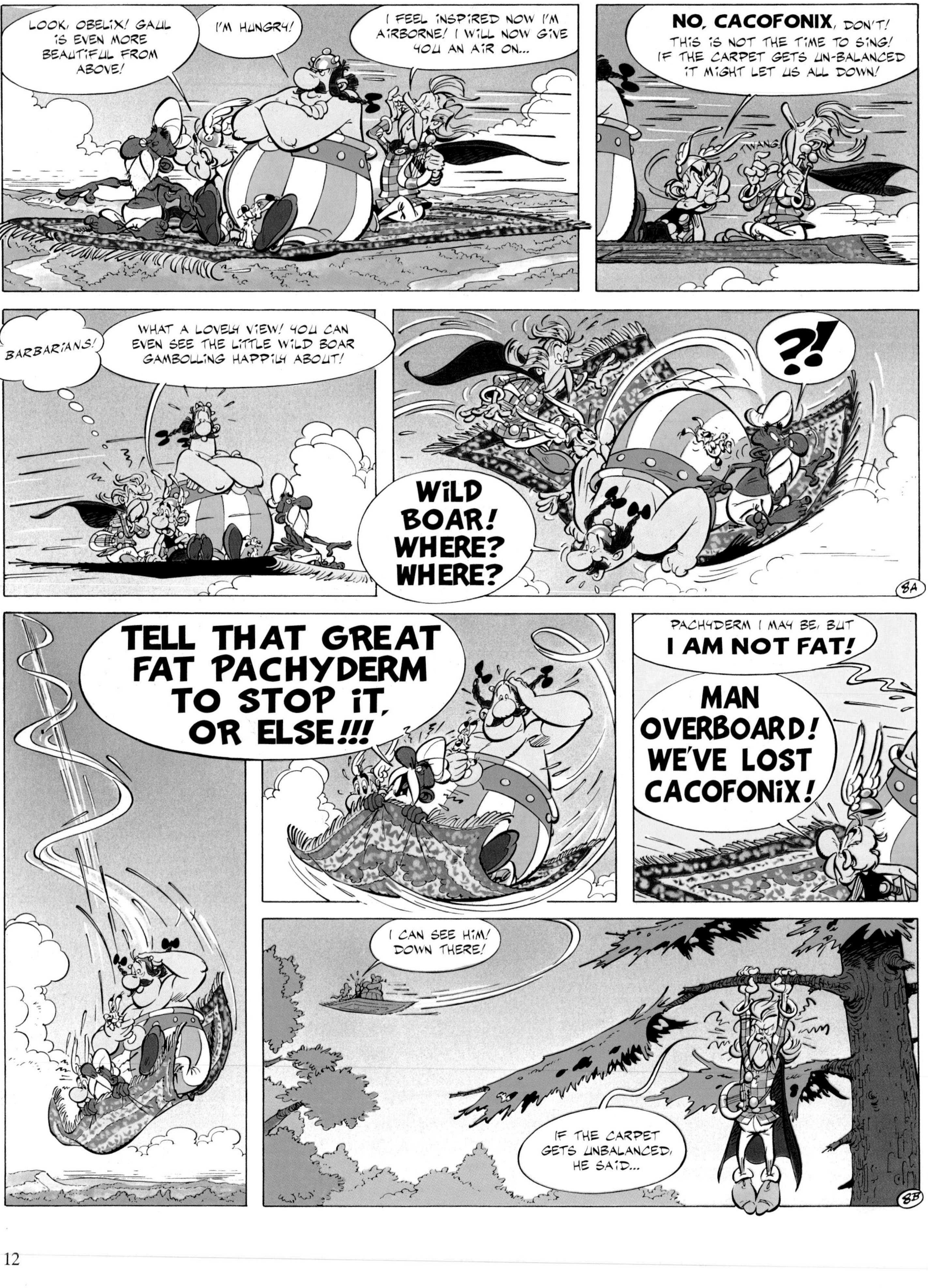
LOOK, OBELIX! GAUL IS EVEN MORE BEAUTIFUL FROM ABOVE!
I'M HUNGRY!
I FEEL INSPIRED NOW I'M AIRBORNE! I WILL NOW GIVE YOU AN AIR ON...
NO, CACOFONIX, DON'T! THIS IS NOT THE TIME TO SING! IF THE CARPET GETS UN-BALANCED IT MIGHT LET US ALL DOWN!
TWANG
BARBARIANS!
WHAT A LOVELY VIEW! YOU CAN EVEN SEE THE LITTLE WILD BOAR GAMBOLLING HAPPILY ABOUT!
WILD BOAR! WHERE? WHERE?
?!
8A
TELL THAT GREAT FAT PACHYDERM TO STOP IT, OR ELSE!!!
PACHYDERM I MAY BE, BUT I AM NOT FAT!
MAN OVERBOARD! WE'VE LOST CACOFONIX!
I CAN SEE HIM! DOWN THERE!
IF THE CARPET GETS UNBALANCED, HE SAID...
8B

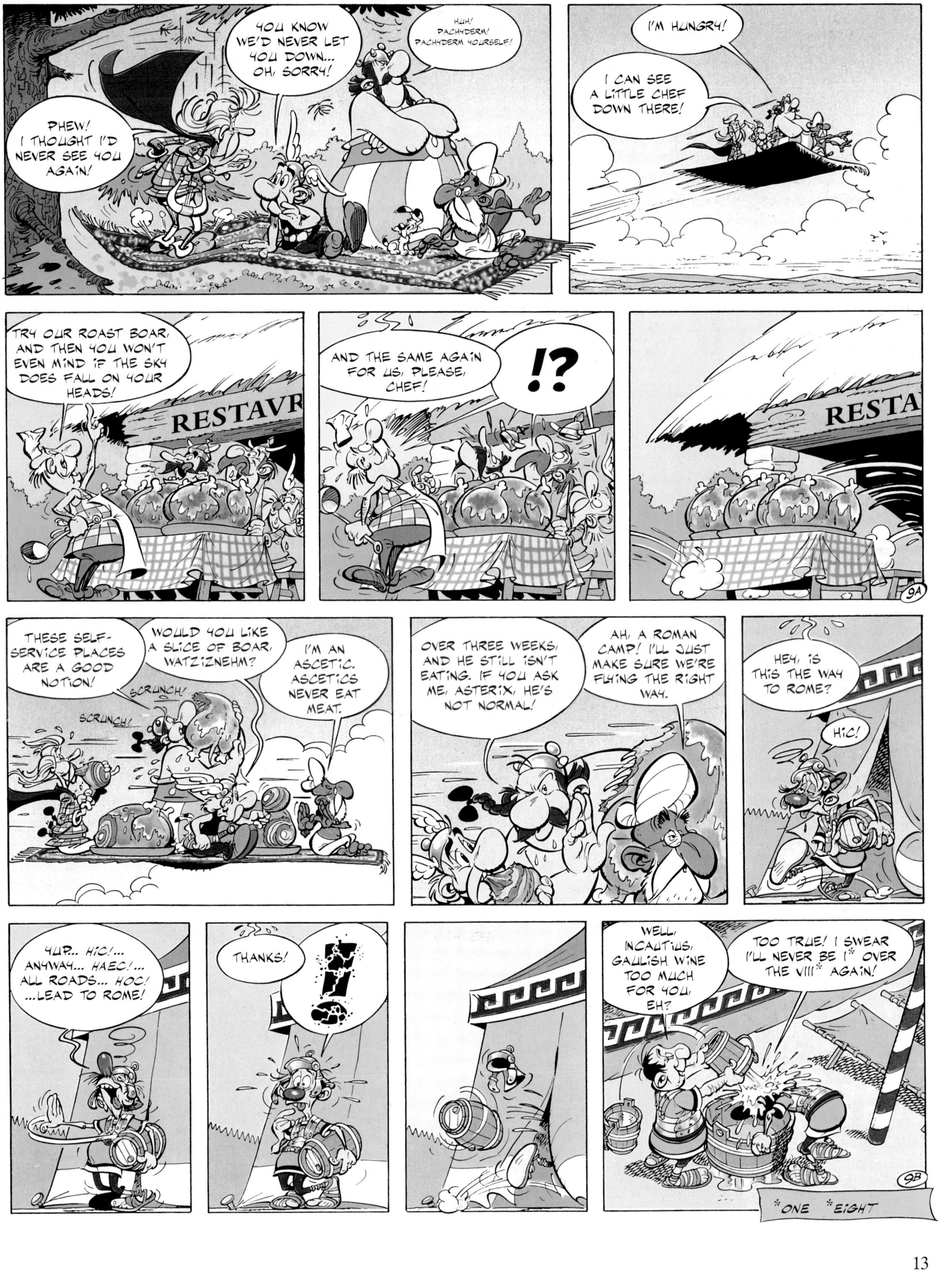
PHEW! I THOUGHT I'D NEVER SEE YOU AGAIN!
YOU KNOW WE'D NEVER LET YOU DOWN... OH, SORRY!
HUH! PACHYDERM! PACHYDERM YOURSELF!
I'M HUNGRY!
I CAN SEE A LITTLE CHEF DOWN THERE!
TRY OUR ROAST BOAR, AND THEN YOU WON'T EVEN MIND IF THE SKY DOES FALL ON YOUR HEADS!
RESTAVR
AND THE SAME AGAIN FOR US, PLEASE, CHEF!
!?
RESTA
9A
THESE SELF-SERVICE PLACES ARE A GOOD NOTION!
WOULD YOU LIKE A SLICE OF BOAR, WATZIZNEHM?
I'M AN ASCETIC. ASCETICS NEVER EAT MEAT.
SCRUNCH!
SCRUNCH!
OVER THREE WEEKS, AND HE STILL ISN'T EATING. IF YOU ASK ME, ASTERIX, HE'S NOT NORMAL!
AH, A ROMAN CAMP! I'LL JUST MAKE SURE WE'RE FLYING THE RIGHT WAY.
HEY, IS THIS THE WAY TO ROME?
HIC!
YUP... HIC!... ANYWAY... HAEC!... ALL ROADS... HOC! ...LEAD TO ROME!
THANKS!
!
WELL, INCAUTIUS, GAULISH WINE TOO MUCH FOR YOU, EH?
TOO TRUE! I SWEAR I'LL NEVER BE I* OVER THE VIII* AGAIN!
9B
*ONE *EIGHT

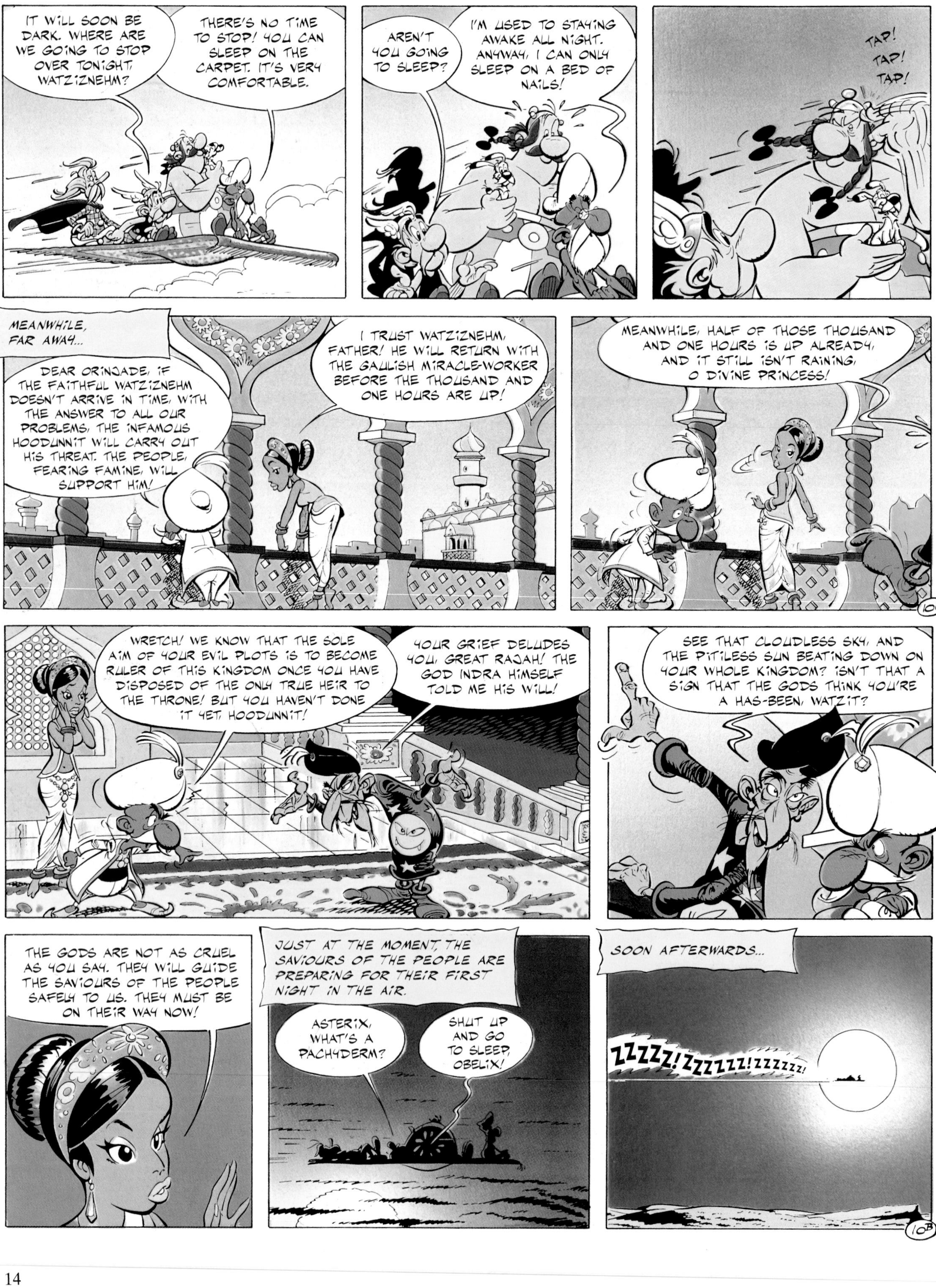
IT WILL SOON BE DARK. WHERE ARE WE GOING TO STOP OVER TONIGHT, WATZIZNEHM?
THERE'S NO TIME TO STOP! YOU CAN SLEEP ON THE CARPET. IT'S VERY COMFORTABLE.
AREN'T YOU GOING TO SLEEP?
I'M USED TO STAYING AWAKE ALL NIGHT. ANYWAY, I CAN ONLY SLEEP ON A BED OF NAILS!
TAP! TAP! TAP!
MEANWHILE, FAR AWAY...
DEAR ORINJADE, IF THE FAITHFUL WATZIZNEHM DOESN'T ARRIVE IN TIME, WITH THE ANSWER TO ALL OUR PROBLEMS, THE INFAMOUS HOODUNNIT WILL CARRY OUT HIS THREAT. THE PEOPLE, FEARING FAMINE, WILL SUPPORT HIM!
I TRUST WATZIZNEHM, FATHER! HE WILL RETURN WITH THE GAULISH MIRACLE-WORKER BEFORE THE THOUSAND AND ONE HOURS ARE UP!
MEANWHILE, HALF OF THOSE THOUSAND AND ONE HOURS IS UP ALREADY, AND IT STILL ISN'T RAINING, O DIVINE PRINCESS!
10A
WRETCH! WE KNOW THAT THE SOLE AIM OF YOUR EVIL PLOTS IS TO BECOME RULER OF THIS KINGDOM ONCE YOU HAVE DISPOSED OF THE ONLY TRUE HEIR TO THE THRONE! BUT YOU HAVEN'T DONE IT YET, HOODUNNIT!
YOUR GRIEF DELUDES YOU, GREAT RAJAH! THE GOD INDRA HIMSELF TOLD ME HIS WILL!
SEE THAT CLOUDLESS SKY, AND THE PITILESS SUN BEATING DOWN ON YOUR WHOLE KINGDOM? ISN'T THAT A SIGN THAT THE GODS THINK YOU'RE A HAS-BEEN, WATZIT?
THE GODS ARE NOT AS CRUEL AS YOU SAY. THEY WILL GUIDE THE SAVIOURS OF THE PEOPLE SAFELY TO US. THEY MUST BE ON THEIR WAY NOW!
JUST AT THE MOMENT, THE SAVIOURS OF THE PEOPLE ARE PREPARING FOR THEIR FIRST NIGHT IN THE AIR.
ASTERIX, WHAT'S A PACHYDERM?
SHUT UP AND GO TO SLEEP, OBELIX!
SOON AFTERWARDS...
ZZZZZ! ZZZZZZ! ZZZZZZZ!
10B

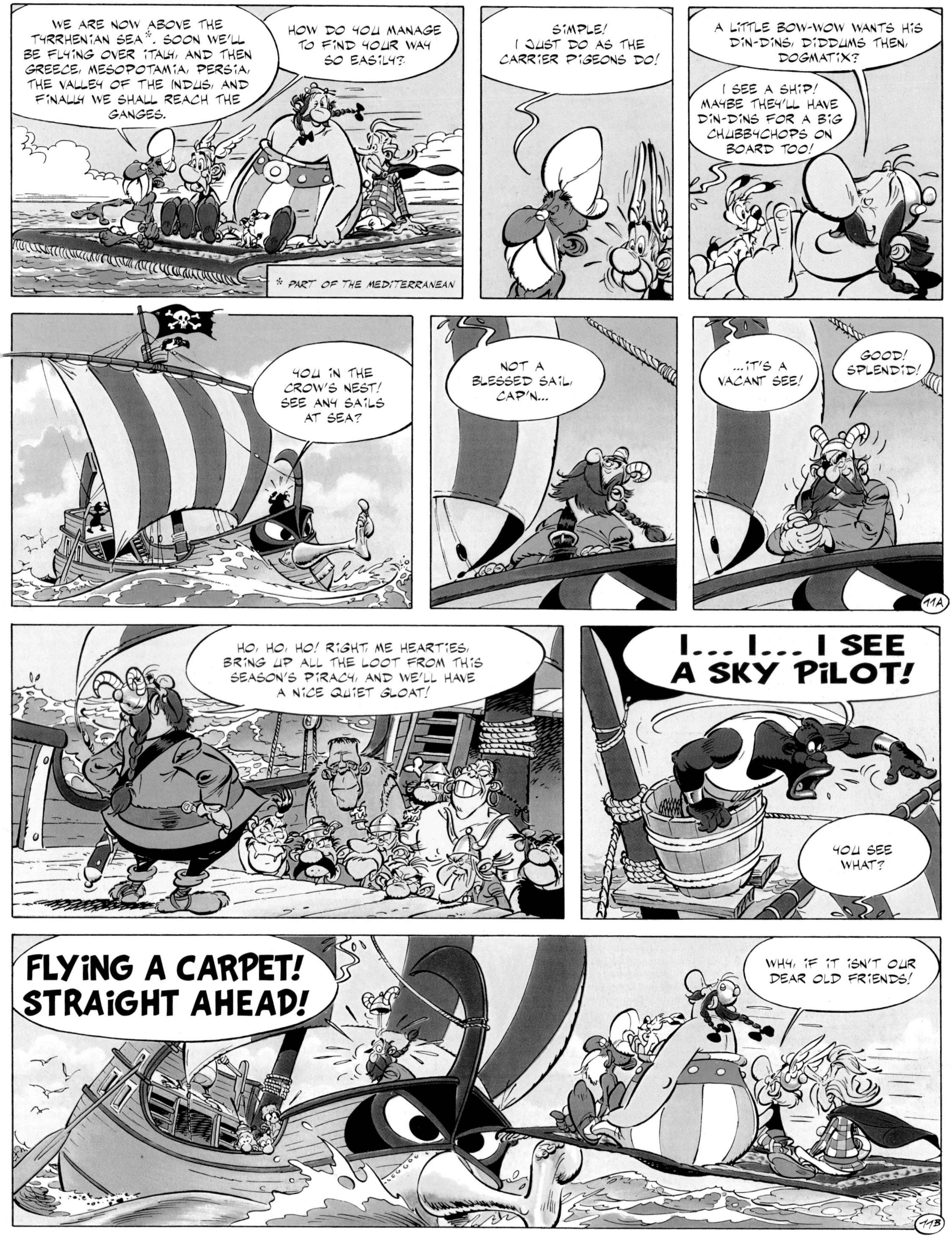
WE ARE NOW ABOVE THE TYRRHENIAN SEA*. SOON WE'LL BE FLYING OVER ITALY, AND THEN GREECE, MESOPOTAMIA, PERSIA, THE VALLEY OF THE INDUS, AND FINALLY WE SHALL REACH THE GANGES.
HOW DO YOU MANAGE TO FIND YOUR WAY SO EASILY?
* PART OF THE MEDITERRANEAN
SIMPLE! I JUST DO AS THE CARRIER PIGEONS DO!
A LITTLE BOW-WOW WANTS HIS DIN-DINS, DIDDUMS THEN, DOGMATIX?
I SEE A SHIP! MAYBE THEY'LL HAVE DIN-DINS FOR A BIG CHUBBYCHOPS ON BOARD TOO!
YOU IN THE CROW'S NEST! SEE ANY SAILS AT SEA?
NOT A BLESSED SAIL, CAP'N...
...IT'S A VACANT SEE!
GOOD! SPLENDID!
11A
HO, HO, HO! RIGHT, ME HEARTIES, BRING UP ALL THE LOOT FROM THIS SEASON'S PIRACY, AND WE'LL HAVE A NICE QUIET GLOAT!
I... I... I SEE A SKY PILOT!
YOU SEE WHAT?
FLYING A CARPET! STRAIGHT AHEAD!
WHY, IF IT ISN'T OUR DEAR OLD FRIENDS!
11B

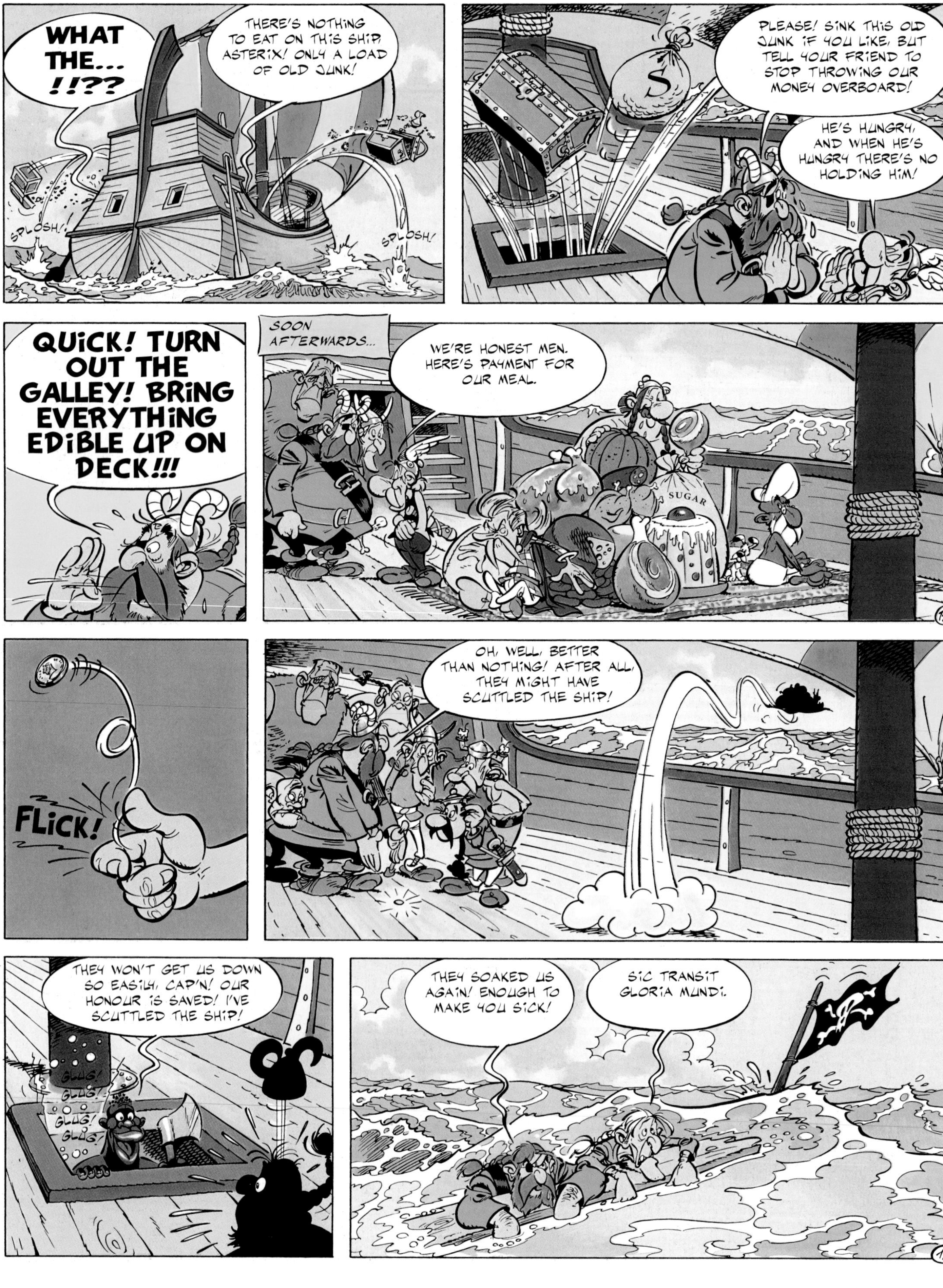
WHAT THE... !!??
THERE'S NOTHING TO EAT ON THIS SHIP, ASTERIX! ONLY A LOAD OF OLD JUNK!
SPLOSH!
SPLOSH!
PLEASE! SINK THIS OLD JUNK IF YOU LIKE, BUT TELL YOUR FRIEND TO STOP THROWING OUR MONEY OVERBOARD!
HE'S HUNGRY, AND WHEN HE'S HUNGRY THERE'S NO HOLDING HIM!
QUICK! TURN OUT THE GALLEY! BRING EVERYTHING EDIBLE UP ON DECK!!!
SOON AFTERWARDS...
WE'RE HONEST MEN. HERE'S PAYMENT FOR OUR MEAL.
SUGAR
FLICK!
OH, WELL, BETTER THAN NOTHING! AFTER ALL, THEY MIGHT HAVE SCUTTLED THE SHIP!
THEY WON'T GET US DOWN SO EASILY, CAP'N! OUR HONOUR IS SAVED! I'VE SCUTTLED THE SHIP!
GLUG! GLUG! GLUG! GLUG!
THEY SOAKED US AGAIN! ENOUGH TO MAKE YOU SICK!
SIC TRANSIT GLORIA MUNDI.

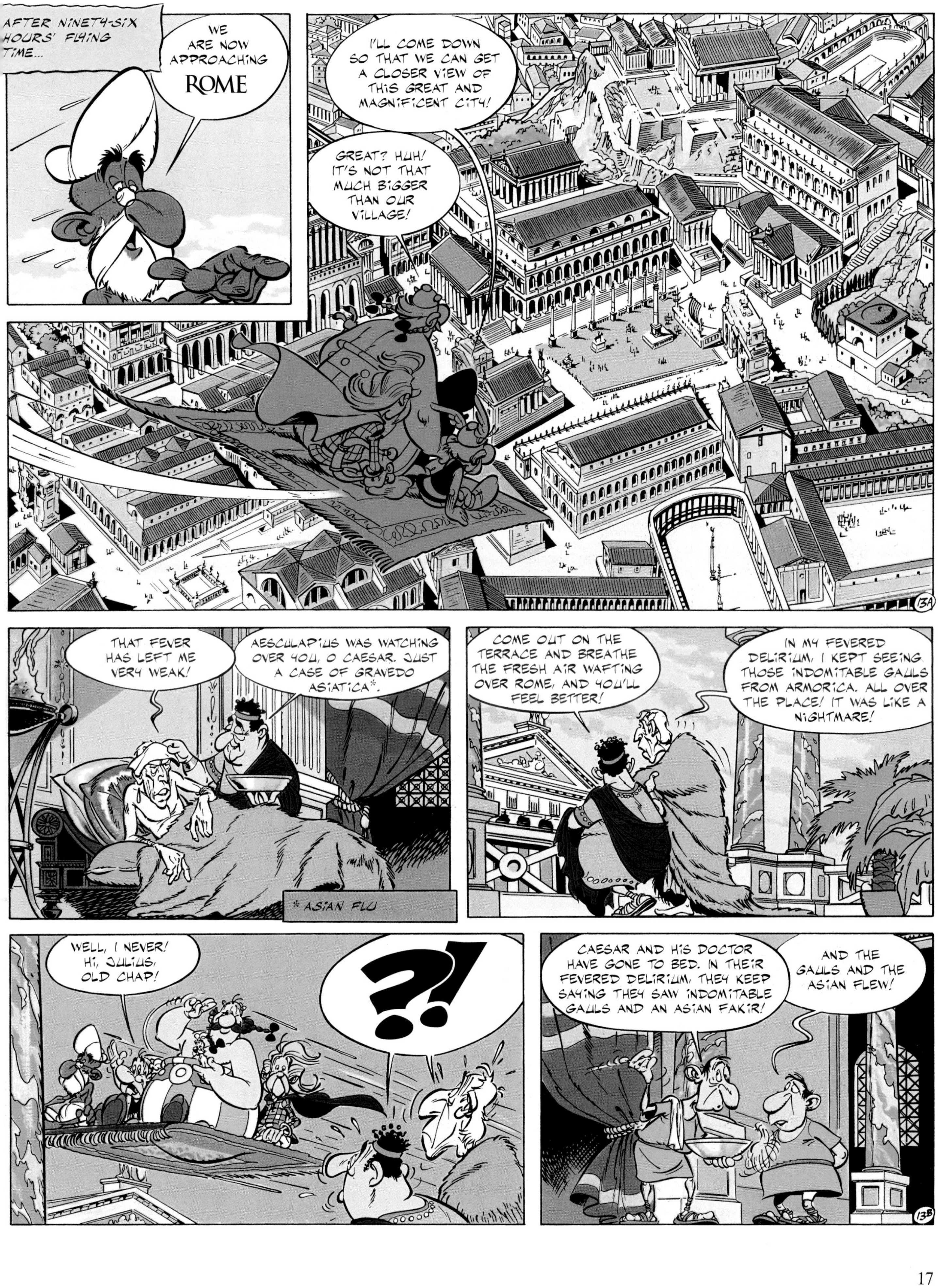
AFTER NINETY-SIX HOURS' FLYING TIME...
WE ARE NOW APPROACHING ROME
I'LL COME DOWN SO THAT WE CAN GET A CLOSER VIEW OF THIS GREAT AND MAGNIFICENT CITY!
GREAT? HUH! IT'S NOT THAT MUCH BIGGER THAN OUR VILLAGE!
THAT FEVER HAS LEFT ME VERY WEAK!
AESCULAPIUS WAS WATCHING OVER YOU, O CAESAR. JUST A CASE OF GRAVEDO ASIATICA*.
* ASIAN FLU
COME OUT ON THE TERRACE AND BREATHE THE FRESH AIR WAFTING OVER ROME, AND YOU'LL FEEL BETTER!
IN MY FEVERED DELIRIUM, I KEPT SEEING THOSE INDOMITABLE GAULS FROM ARMORICA. ALL OVER THE PLACE! IT WAS LIKE A NIGHTMARE!
WELL, I NEVER! HI, JULIUS, OLD CHAP!
?!
CAESAR AND HIS DOCTOR HAVE GONE TO BED. IN THEIR FEVERED DELIRIUM, THEY KEEP SAYING THEY SAW INDOMITABLE GAULS AND AN ASIAN FAKIR!
AND THE GAULS AND THE ASIAN FLEW!

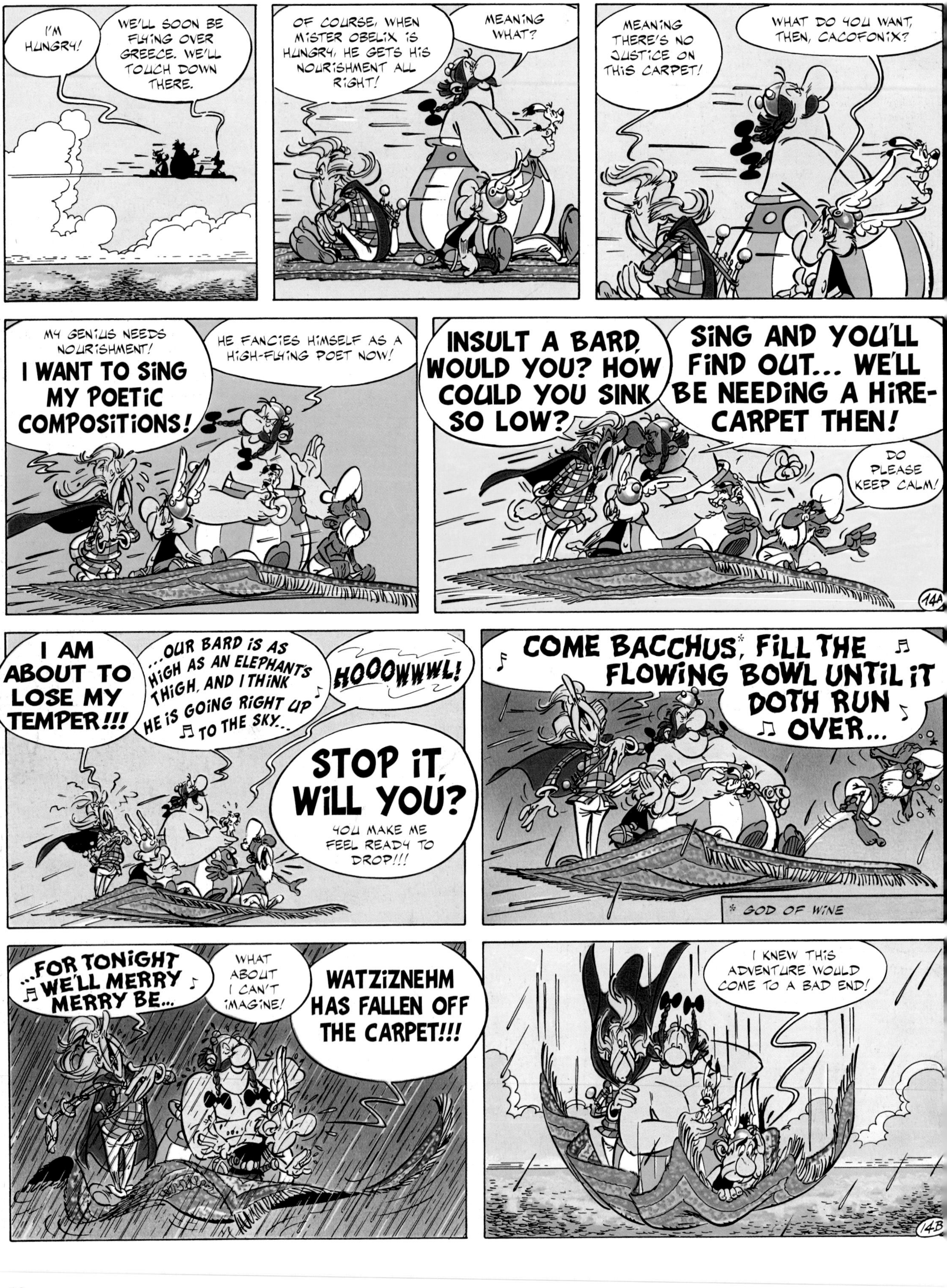
I'M HUNGRY!
WE'LL SOON BE FLYING OVER GREECE. WE'LL TOUCH DOWN THERE.
OF COURSE, WHEN MISTER OBELIX IS HUNGRY, HE GETS HIS NOURISHMENT ALL RIGHT!
MEANING WHAT?
MEANING THERE'S NO JUSTICE ON THIS CARPET!
WHAT DO YOU WANT, THEN, CACOFONIX?
MY GENIUS NEEDS NOURISHMENT! I WANT TO SING MY POETIC COMPOSITIONS!
HE FANCIES HIMSELF AS A HIGH-FLYING POET NOW!
INSULT A BARD, WOULD YOU? HOW COULD YOU SINK SO LOW?
SING AND YOU'LL FIND OUT... WE'LL BE NEEDING A HIRE-CARPET THEN!
DO PLEASE KEEP CALM!
14A
I AM ABOUT TO LOSE MY TEMPER!!!
...OUR BARD IS AS HIGH AS AN ELEPHANT'S THIGH, AND I THINK HE IS GOING RIGHT UP TO THE SKY...
HOOOWWWL!
STOP IT, WILL YOU?
YOU MAKE ME FEEL READY TO DROP!!!
COME BACCHUS*, FILL THE FLOWING BOWL UNTIL IT DOTH RUN OVER...
* GOD OF WINE
...FOR TONIGHT WE'LL MERRY MERRY BE...
WHAT ABOUT I CAN'T IMAGINE!
WATZIZNEHM HAS FALLEN OFF THE CARPET!!!
I KNEW THIS ADVENTURE WOULD COME TO A BAD END!
14B

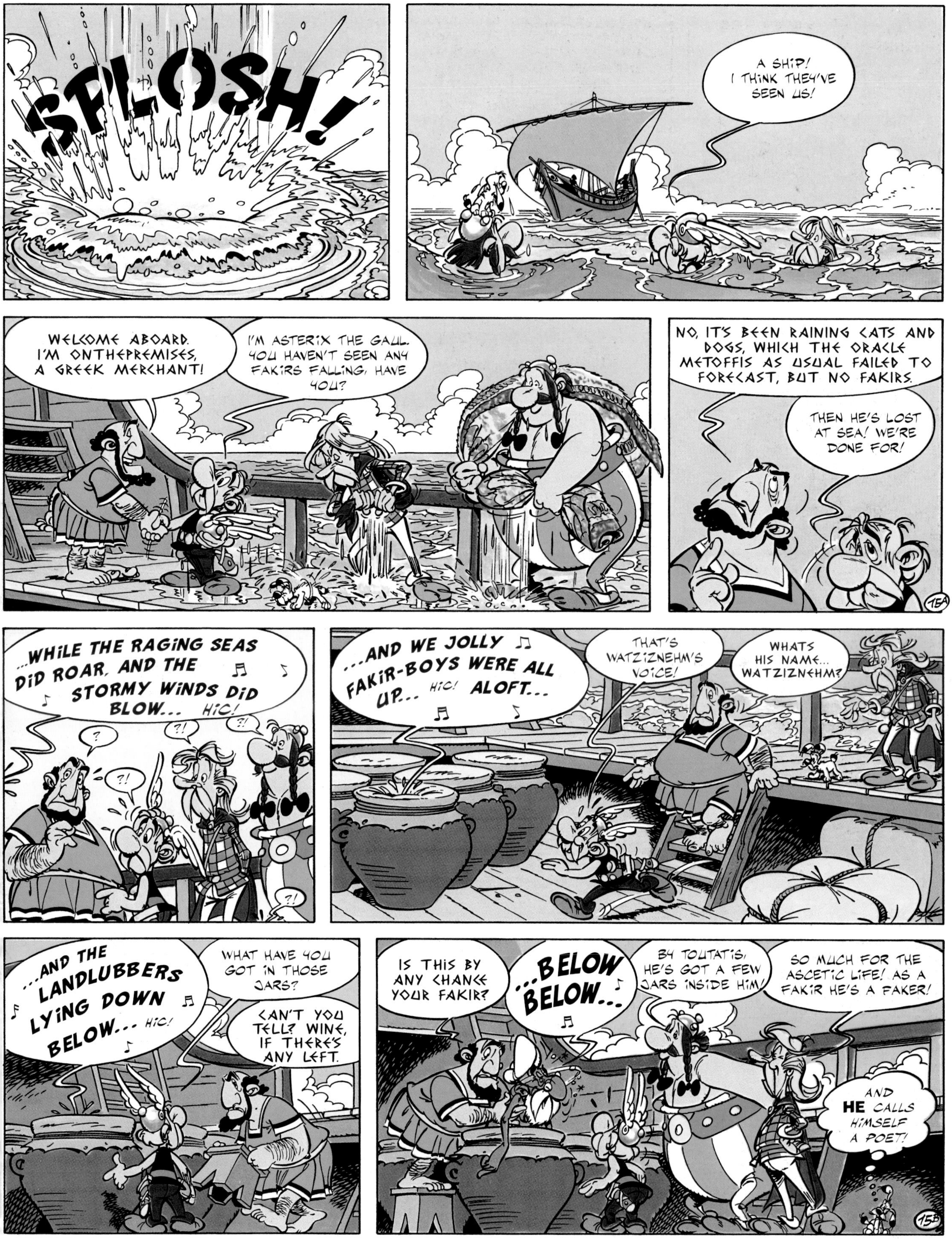
SPLOSH!
A SHIP! I THINK THEY'VE SEEN US!
WELCOME ABOARD. I'M ONTHEPREMISES, A GREEK MERCHANT!
I'M ASTERIX THE GAUL. YOU HAVEN'T SEEN ANY FAKIRS FALLING, HAVE YOU?
NO, IT'S BEEN RAINING CATS AND DOGS, WHICH THE ORACLE METOFFIS AS USUAL FAILED TO FORECAST, BUT NO FAKIRS.
THEN HE'S LOST AT SEA! WE'RE DONE FOR!
...WHILE THE RAGING SEAS DID ROAR, AND THE STORMY WINDS DID BLOW... HIC!
?
?!
?!
?!
?!
...AND WE JOLLY FAKIR-BOYS WERE ALL UP... HIC! ALOFT...
THAT'S WATZIZNEHM'S VOICE!
WHATS HIS NAME... WATZIZNEHM?
...AND THE LANDLUBBERS LYING DOWN BELOW... HIC!
WHAT HAVE YOU GOT IN THOSE JARS?
CAN'T YOU TELL? WINE, IF THERE'S ANY LEFT.
IS THIS BY ANY CHANCE YOUR FAKIR?
...BELOW BELOW...
BY TOUTATIS, HE'S GOT A FEW JARS INSIDE HIM!
SO MUCH FOR THE ASCETIC LIFE! AS A FAKIR HE'S A FAKER!
AND HE CALLS HIMSELF A POET!

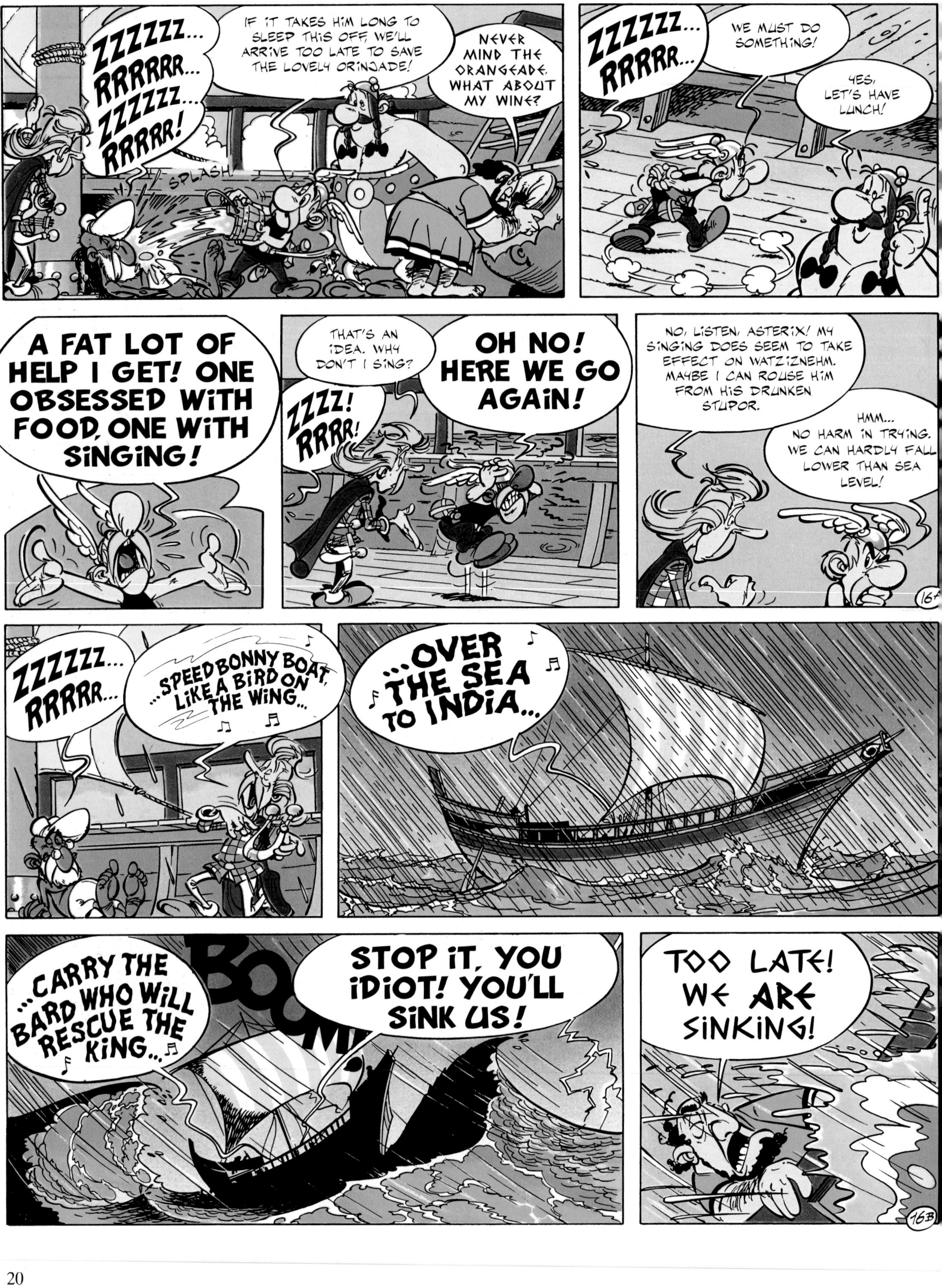

ZZZZZZ... RRRRRR... ZZZZZZ... RRRRR!
SPLASH!
IF IT TAKES HIM LONG TO SLEEP THIS OFF, WE'LL ARRIVE TOO LATE TO SAVE THE LOVELY ORINJADE!
NEVER MIND THE ORANGEADE. WHAT ABOUT MY WINE?
ZZZZZZ... RRRRR...
WE MUST DO SOMETHING!
YES, LET'S HAVE LUNCH!
A FAT LOT OF HELP I GET! ONE OBSESSED WITH FOOD, ONE WITH SINGING!
ZZZZ! RRRR!
THAT'S AN IDEA. WHY DON'T I SING?
OH NO! HERE WE GO AGAIN!
NO, LISTEN, ASTERIX! MY SINGING DOES SEEM TO TAKE EFFECT ON WATZIZNEHM. MAYBE I CAN ROUSE HIM FROM HIS DRUNKEN STUPOR.
HMM... NO HARM IN TRYING. WE CAN HARDLY FALL LOWER THAN SEA LEVEL!
ZZZZZZ... RRRRR...
...SPEED BONNY BOAT, LIKE A BIRD ON THE WING...
...OVER THE SEA TO INDIA...
...CARRY THE BARD WHO WILL RESCUE THE KING...
BOOM!
STOP IT, YOU IDIOT! YOU'LL SINK US!
TOO LATE! WE ARE SINKING!
16B

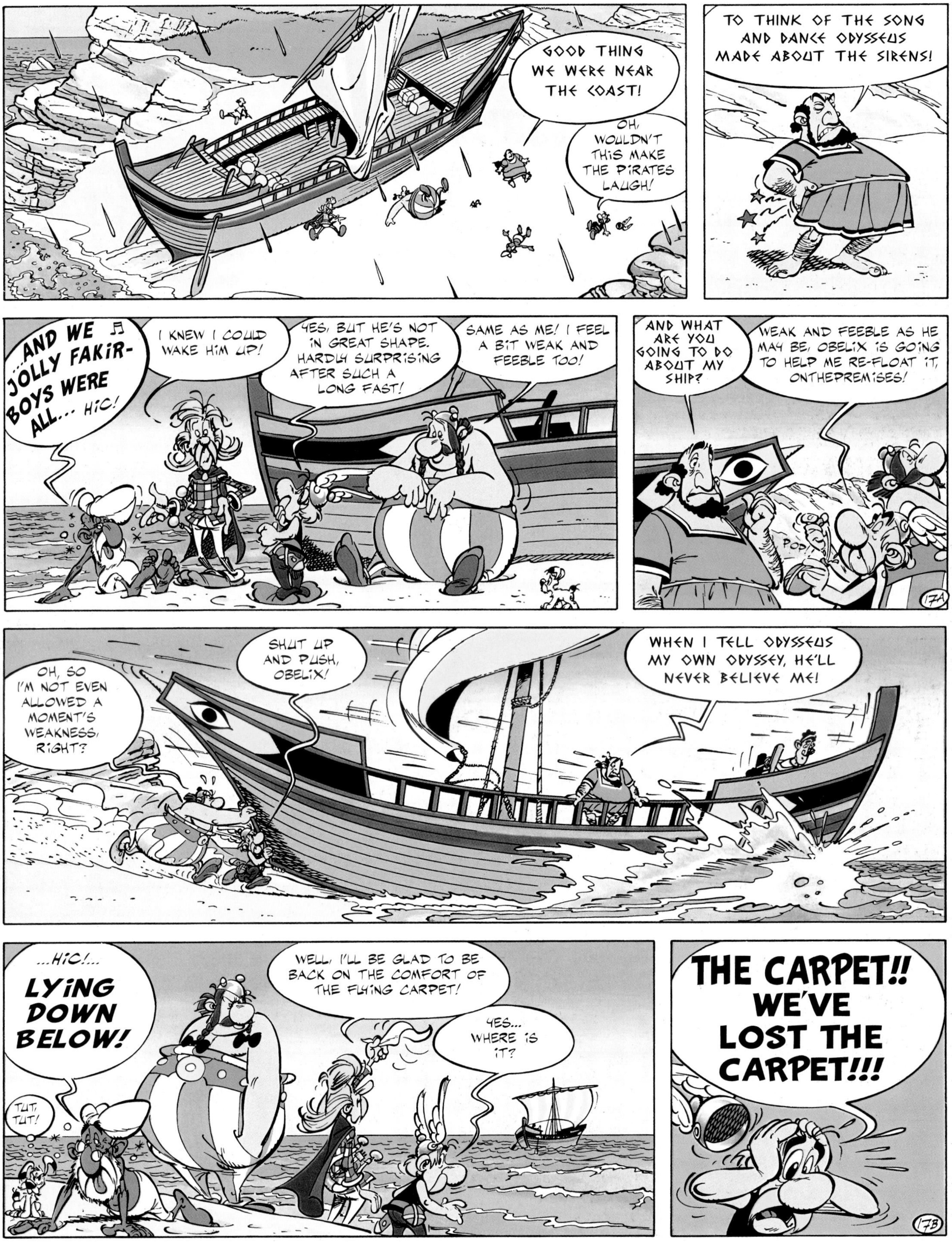
GOOD THING WE WERE NEAR THE COAST!
OH, WOULDN'T THIS MAKE THE PIRATES LAUGH!
TO THINK OF THE SONG AND DANCE ODYSSEUS MADE ABOUT THE SIRENS!
...AND WE JOLLY FAKIR-BOYS WERE ALL... HIC!
I KNEW I COULD WAKE HIM UP!
YES, BUT HE'S NOT IN GREAT SHAPE. HARDLY SURPRISING AFTER SUCH A LONG FAST!
SAME AS ME! I FEEL A BIT WEAK AND FEEBLE TOO!
AND WHAT ARE YOU GOING TO DO ABOUT MY SHIP?
WEAK AND FEEBLE AS HE MAY BE, OBELIX IS GOING TO HELP ME RE-FLOAT IT, ONTHEPREMISES!
POP!
17A
OH, SO I'M NOT EVEN ALLOWED A MOMENT'S WEAKNESS, RIGHT?
SHUT UP AND PUSH, OBELIX!
WHEN I TELL ODYSSEUS MY OWN ODYSSEY, HE'LL NEVER BELIEVE ME!
...HIC!... LYING DOWN BELOW!
TUT, TUT!
WELL, I'LL BE GLAD TO BE BACK ON THE COMFORT OF THE FLYING CARPET!
YES... WHERE IS IT?
THE CARPET!! WE'VE LOST THE CARPET!!!
17B

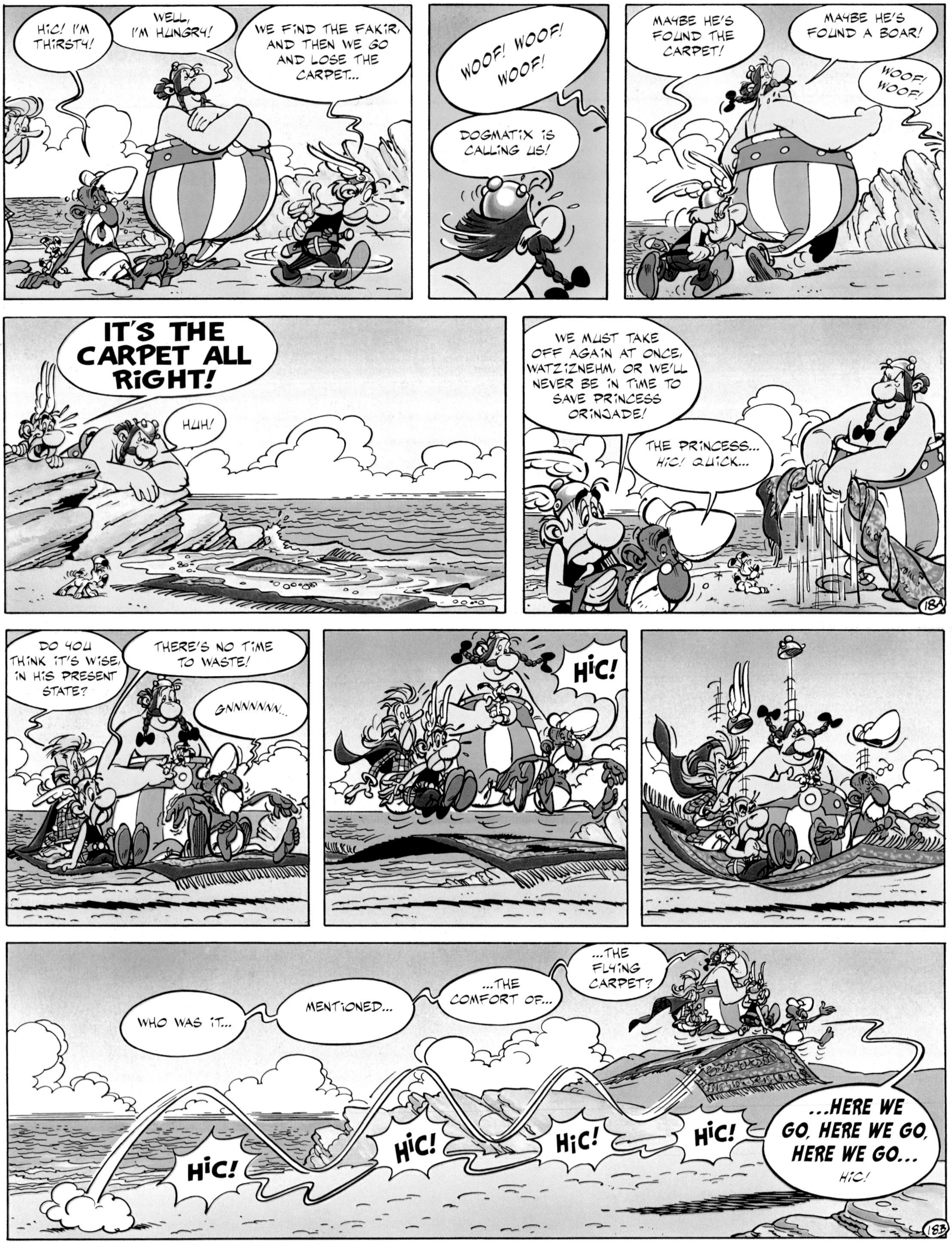
HIC! I'M THIRSTY!
WELL, I'M HUNGRY!
WE FIND THE FAKIR, AND THEN WE GO AND LOSE THE CARPET...
WOOF! WOOF! WOOF!
DOGMATIX IS CALLING US!
MAYBE HE'S FOUND THE CARPET!
MAYBE HE'S FOUND A BOAR!
WOOF! WOOF!
IT'S THE CARPET ALL RIGHT!
HUH!
WE MUST TAKE OFF AGAIN AT ONCE, WATZIZNEHM, OR WE'LL NEVER BE IN TIME TO SAVE PRINCESS ORINJADE!
THE PRINCESS... HIC! QUICK...
DO YOU THINK IT'S WISE, IN HIS PRESENT STATE?
THERE'S NO TIME TO WASTE!
GNNNNNNN...
HIC!
WHO WAS IT...
MENTIONED...
...THE COMFORT OF...
...THE FLYING CARPET?
HIC!
HIC!
HIC!
HIC!
...HERE WE GO, HERE WE GO, HERE WE GO...
HIC!

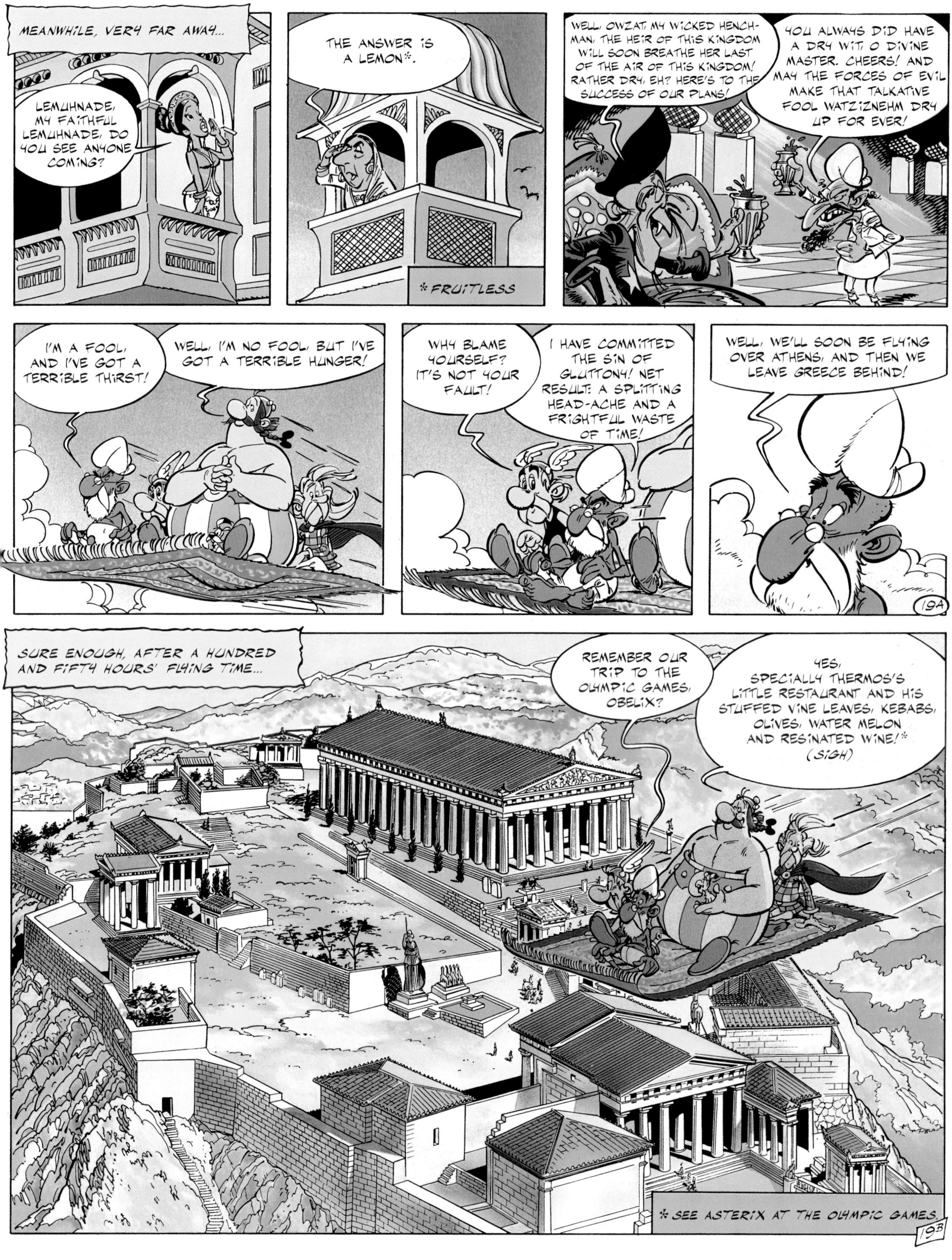
MEANWHILE, VERY FAR AWAY...
LEMUHNADE, MY FAITHFUL LEMUHNADE, DO YOU SEE ANYONE COMING?
THE ANSWER IS A LEMON*.
* FRUITLESS
WELL, OWZAT, MY WICKED HENCHMAN, THE HEIR OF THIS KINGDOM WILL SOON BREATHE HER LAST OF THE AIR OF THIS KINGDOM! RATHER DRY, EH? HERE'S TO THE SUCCESS OF OUR PLANS!
YOU ALWAYS DID HAVE A DRY WIT, O DIVINE MASTER. CHEERS! AND MAY THE FORCES OF EVIL MAKE THAT TALKATIVE FOOL WATZIZNEHM DRY UP FOR EVER!
I'M A FOOL, AND I'VE GOT A TERRIBLE THIRST!
WELL, I'M NO FOOL, BUT I'VE GOT A TERRIBLE HUNGER!
WHY BLAME YOURSELF? IT'S NOT YOUR FAULT!
I HAVE COMMITTED THE SIN OF GLUTTONY! NET RESULT: A SPLITTING HEAD-ACHE AND A FRIGHTFUL WASTE OF TIME!
WELL, WE'LL SOON BE FLYING OVER ATHENS, AND THEN WE LEAVE GREECE BEHIND!
19A
SURE ENOUGH, AFTER A HUNDRED AND FIFTY HOURS' FLYING TIME...
REMEMBER OUR TRIP TO THE OLYMPIC GAMES, OBELIX?
YES, SPECIALLY THERMOS'S LITTLE RESTAURANT AND HIS STUFFED VINE LEAVES, KEBABS, OLIVES, WATER MELON AND RESINATED WINE!* (SIGH)
* SEE ASTERIX AT THE OLYMPIC GAMES.
19B

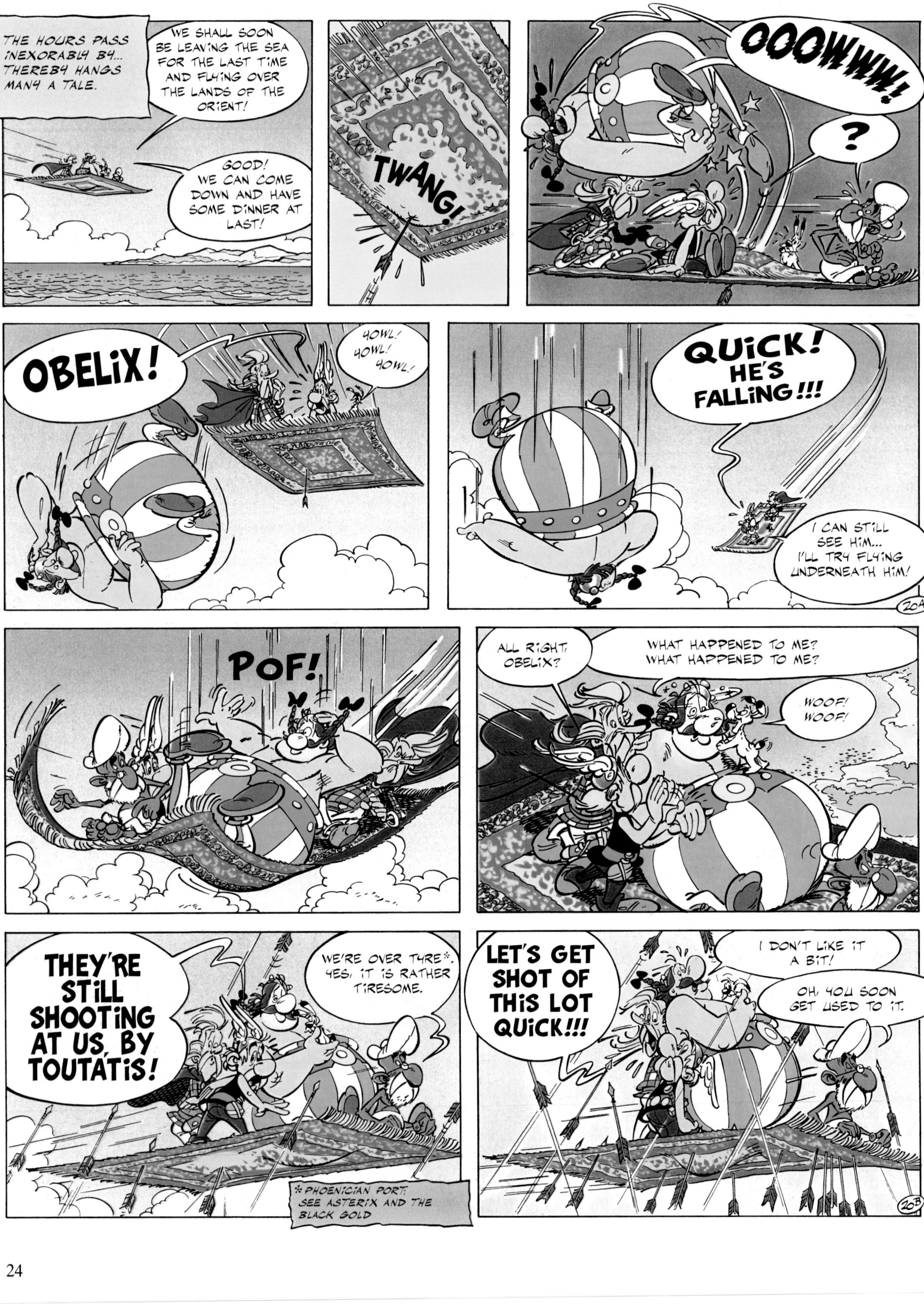
THE HOURS PASS INEXORABLY BY... THEREBY HANGS MANY A TALE.
WE SHALL SOON BE LEAVING THE SEA FOR THE LAST TIME AND FLYING OVER THE LANDS OF THE ORIENT!
GOOD! WE CAN COME DOWN AND HAVE SOME DINNER AT LAST!
TWANG!
OOOWWW!
?
OBELIX!
YOWL! YOWL! YOWL!
QUICK! HE'S FALLING!!!
I CAN STILL SEE HIM... I'LL TRY FLYING UNDERNEATH HIM!
POF!
ALL RIGHT, OBELIX?
WHAT HAPPENED TO ME? WHAT HAPPENED TO ME?
WOOF! WOOF!
THEY'RE STILL SHOOTING AT US, BY TOUTATIS!
WE'RE OVER TYRE*. YES, IT IS RATHER TIRESOME.
*PHOENICIAN PORT. SEE ASTERIX AND THE BLACK GOLD
LET'S GET SHOT OF THIS LOT QUICK!!!
I DON'T LIKE IT A BIT!
OH, YOU SOON GET USED TO IT.

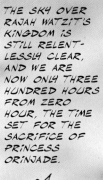

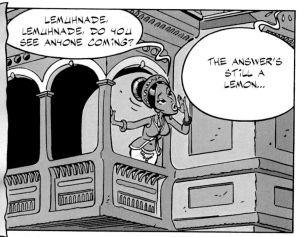

THE SKY OVER RAJAH WATZIT'S KINGDOM IS STILL RELENTLESSLY CLEAR, AND WE ARE NOW ONLY THREE HUNDRED HOURS FROM ZERO HOUR, THE TIME SET FOR THE SACRIFICE OF PRINCESS ORINJADE.
LEMUHNADE, LEMUHNADE, DO YOU SEE ANYONE COMING?
THE ANSWER'S STILL A LEMON...
YOUR WEATHER FORECASTS HAVE BEEN ACCURATE SO FAR, OWZAT! NOT A CLOUD ON THE HORIZON. BUT SUPPOSE WATZIZNEHM BRINGS THAT GAUL BACK IN TIME TO MAKE IT RAIN?
I DON'T BELIEVE IN THAT KIND OF MIRACLE, O DIVINE MASTER. FLYING CARPETS ARE ONE THING, BUT RAIN-MAKING IS SHEER SCIENCE FICTION!
I'M HUNGRY!
SIGH!
FOR YOUR INFORMATION, WE ARE NOW FLYING OVER PERSIA, AND TELL YOUR FRIEND HE MUST LIVE ON HIS HUMP A LITTLE LONGER. WE'VE NO TIME TO WASTE!
EATING IS NEVER A WASTE OF TIME! ARE YOU SURPRISED I'VE GOT THE HUMP?
?
21A
LOOK, IT'S NOTHING WHATEVER TO DO WITH ME!!!
CRASH
WATCH OUT! THE CARPET'S ON FIRE!
THE CARPET'S BEEN HOLED! I CAN'T HOLD IT STEADY!
21B

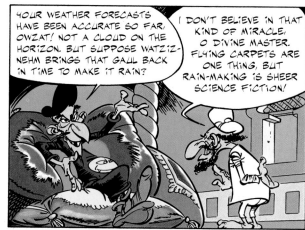

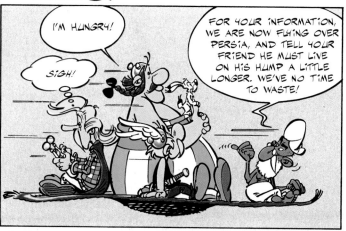

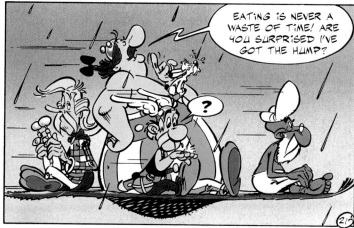

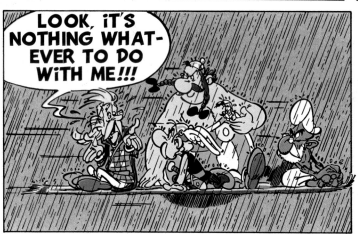

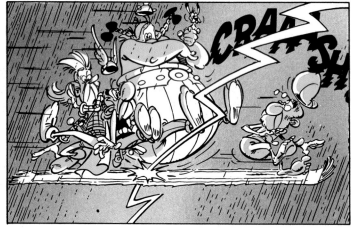

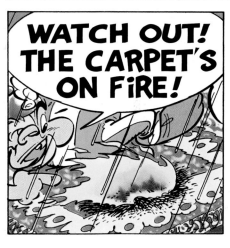

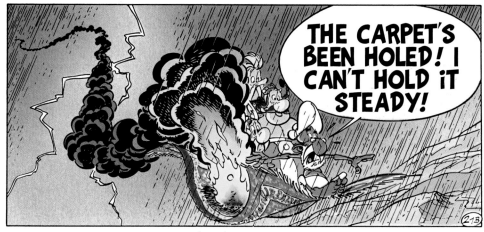

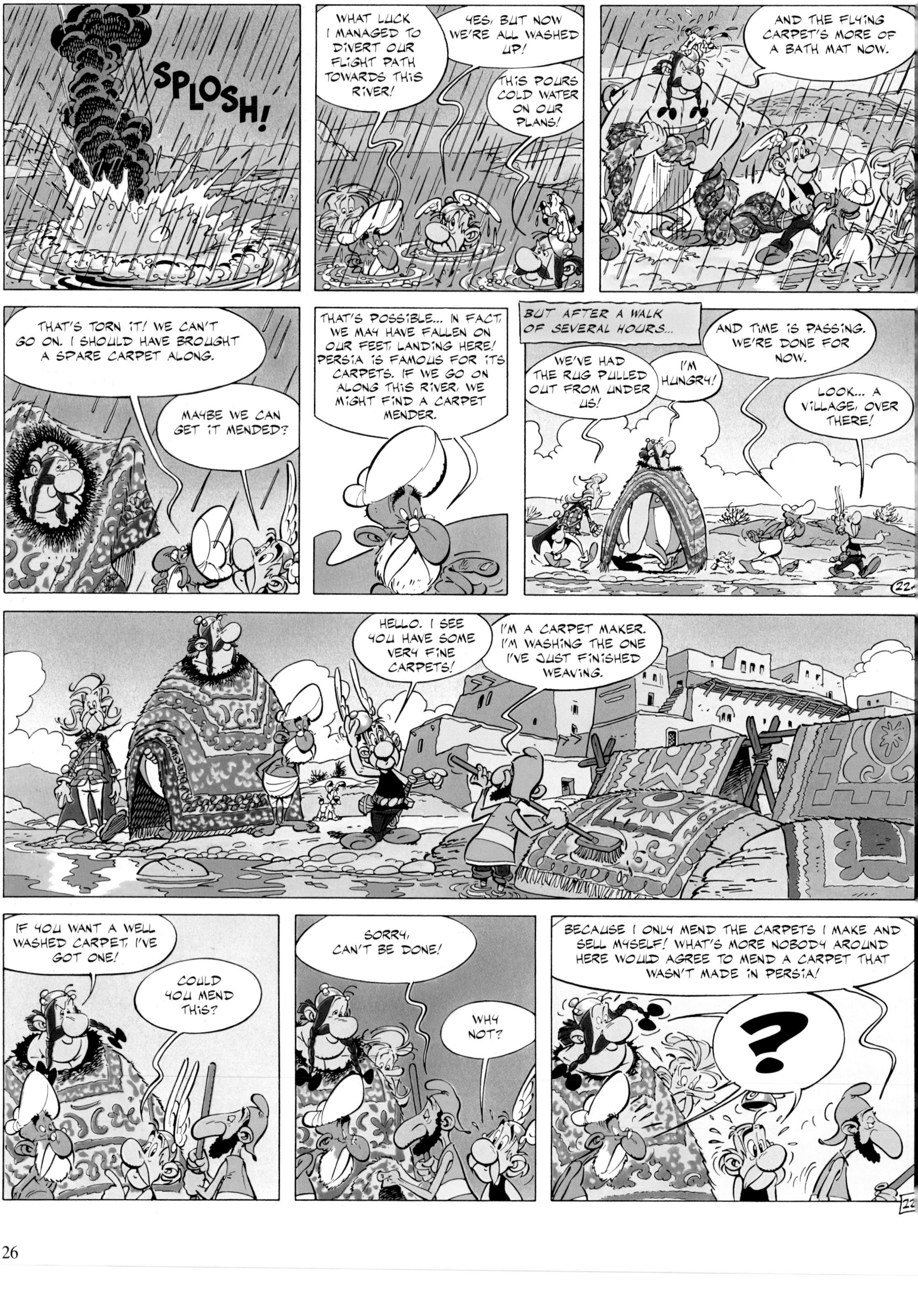
SPLOSH!
WHAT LUCK I MANAGED TO DIVERT OUR FLIGHT PATH TOWARDS THIS RIVER!
YES, BUT NOW WE'RE ALL WASHED UP!
THIS POURS COLD WATER ON OUR PLANS!
AND THE FLYING CARPET'S MORE OF A BATH MAT NOW.
THAT'S TORN IT! WE CAN'T GO ON. I SHOULD HAVE BROUGHT A SPARE CARPET ALONG.
MAYBE WE CAN GET IT MENDED?
THAT'S POSSIBLE... IN FACT, WE MAY HAVE FALLEN ON OUR FEET, LANDING HERE! PERSIA IS FAMOUS FOR ITS CARPETS. IF WE GO ON ALONG THIS RIVER, WE MIGHT FIND A CARPET MENDER.
BUT AFTER A WALK OF SEVERAL HOURS...
WE'VE HAD THE RUG PULLED OUT FROM UNDER US!
I'M HUNGRY!
AND TIME IS PASSING. WE'RE DONE FOR NOW.
LOOK... A VILLAGE, OVER THERE!
HELLO. I SEE YOU HAVE SOME VERY FINE CARPETS!
I'M A CARPET MAKER. I'M WASHING THE ONE I'VE JUST FINISHED WEAVING.
IF YOU WANT A WELL WASHED CARPET, I'VE GOT ONE!
COULD YOU MEND THIS?
SORRY, CAN'T BE DONE!
WHY NOT?
BECAUSE I ONLY MEND THE CARPETS I MAKE AND SELL MYSELF! WHAT'S MORE NOBODY AROUND HERE WOULD AGREE TO MEND A CARPET THAT WASN'T MADE IN PERSIA!
?

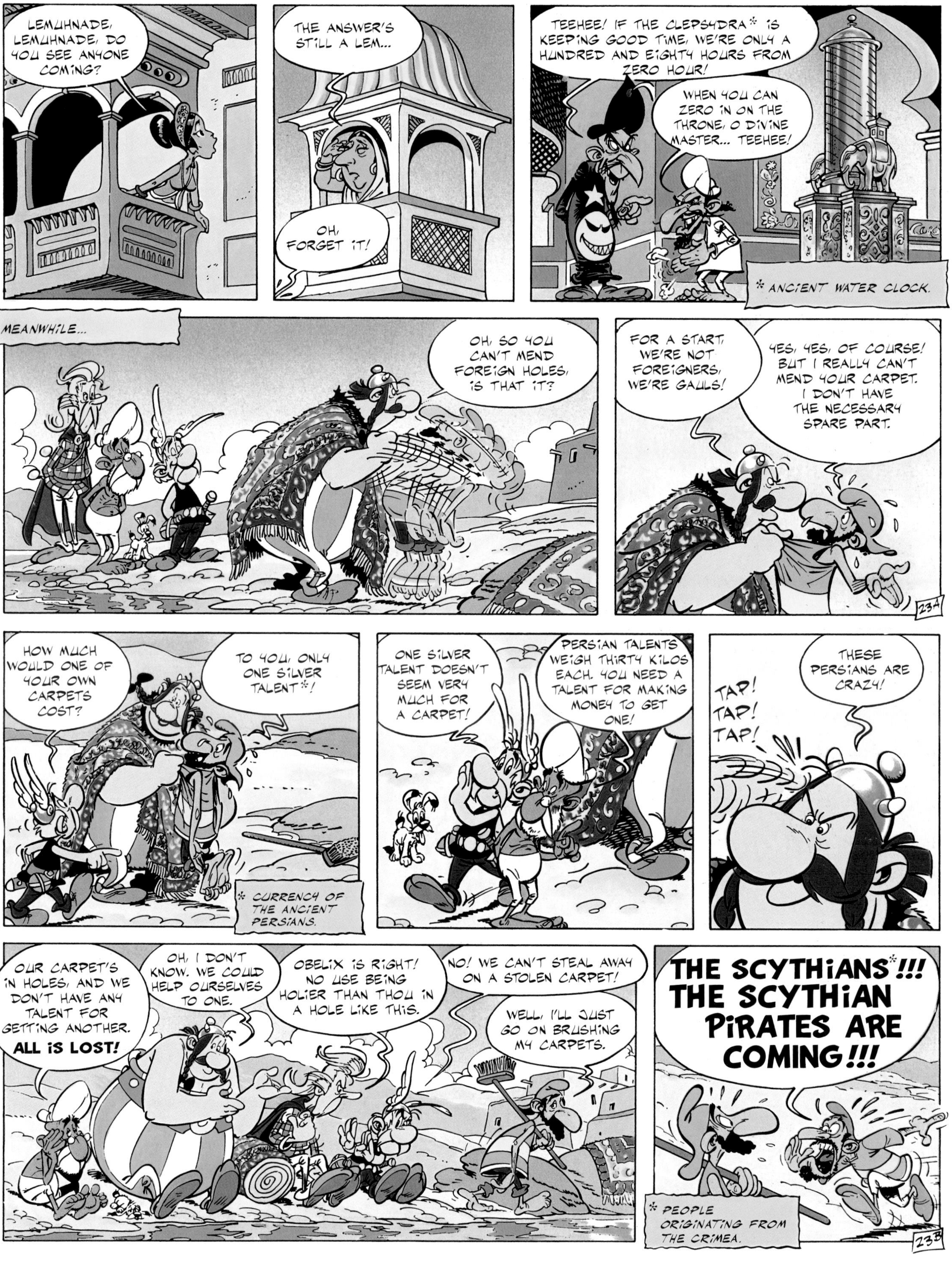
LEMUHNADE, LEMUHNADE, DO YOU SEE ANYONE COMING?
THE ANSWER'S STILL A LEM...
OH, FORGET IT!
TEEHEE! IF THE CLEPSYDRA* IS KEEPING GOOD TIME, WE'RE ONLY A HUNDRED AND EIGHTY HOURS FROM ZERO HOUR!
WHEN YOU CAN ZERO IN ON THE THRONE, O DIVINE MASTER... TEEHEE!
* ANCIENT WATER CLOCK.
MEANWHILE...
OH, SO YOU CAN'T MEND FOREIGN HOLES, IS THAT IT?
FOR A START, WE'RE NOT FOREIGNERS, WE'RE GAULS!
YES, YES, OF COURSE! BUT I REALLY CAN'T MEND YOUR CARPET. I DON'T HAVE THE NECESSARY SPARE PART.
23A
HOW MUCH WOULD ONE OF YOUR OWN CARPETS COST?
TO YOU, ONLY ONE SILVER TALENT*!
* CURRENCY OF THE ANCIENT PERSIANS.
ONE SILVER TALENT DOESN'T SEEM VERY MUCH FOR A CARPET!
PERSIAN TALENTS WEIGH THIRTY KILOS EACH. YOU NEED A TALENT FOR MAKING MONEY TO GET ONE!
TAP! TAP! TAP!
THESE PERSIANS ARE CRAZY!
OUR CARPET'S IN HOLES, AND WE DON'T HAVE ANY TALENT FOR GETTING ANOTHER. ALL IS LOST!
OH, I DON'T KNOW. WE COULD HELP OURSELVES TO ONE.
OBELIX IS RIGHT! NO USE BEING HOLIER THAN THOU IN A HOLE LIKE THIS.
NO! WE CAN'T STEAL AWAY ON A STOLEN CARPET!
WELL, I'LL JUST GO ON BRUSHING MY CARPETS.
THE SCYTHIANS*!!! THE SCYTHIAN PIRATES ARE COMING!!!
* PEOPLE ORIGINATING FROM THE CRIMEA.
23B

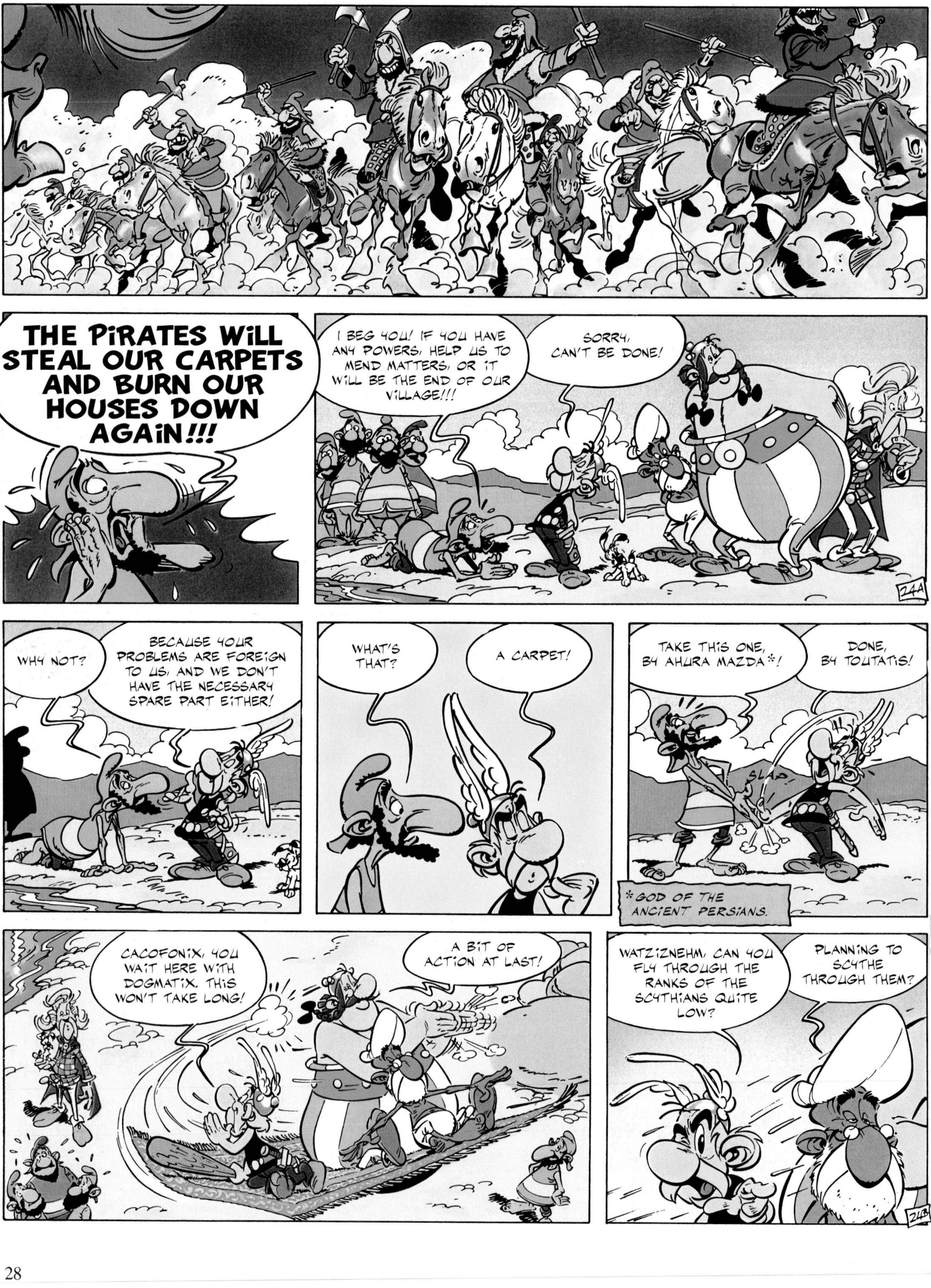
THE PIRATES WILL STEAL OUR CARPETS AND BURN OUR HOUSES DOWN AGAIN!!!
I BEG YOU! IF YOU HAVE ANY POWERS, HELP US TO MEND MATTERS, OR IT WILL BE THE END OF OUR VILLAGE!!!
SORRY, CAN'T BE DONE!
24A
WHY NOT?
BECAUSE YOUR PROBLEMS ARE FOREIGN TO US, AND WE DON'T HAVE THE NECESSARY SPARE PART EITHER!
WHAT'S THAT?
A CARPET!
TAKE THIS ONE, BY AHURA MAZDA*!
DONE, BY TOUTATIS!
SLAP
*GOD OF THE ANCIENT PERSIANS.
CACOFONIX, YOU WAIT HERE WITH DOGMATIX. THIS WON'T TAKE LONG!
A BIT OF ACTION AT LAST!
WATZIZNEHM, CAN YOU FLY THROUGH THE RANKS OF THE SCYTHIANS QUITE LOW?
PLANNING TO SCYTHE THROUGH THEM?
24B

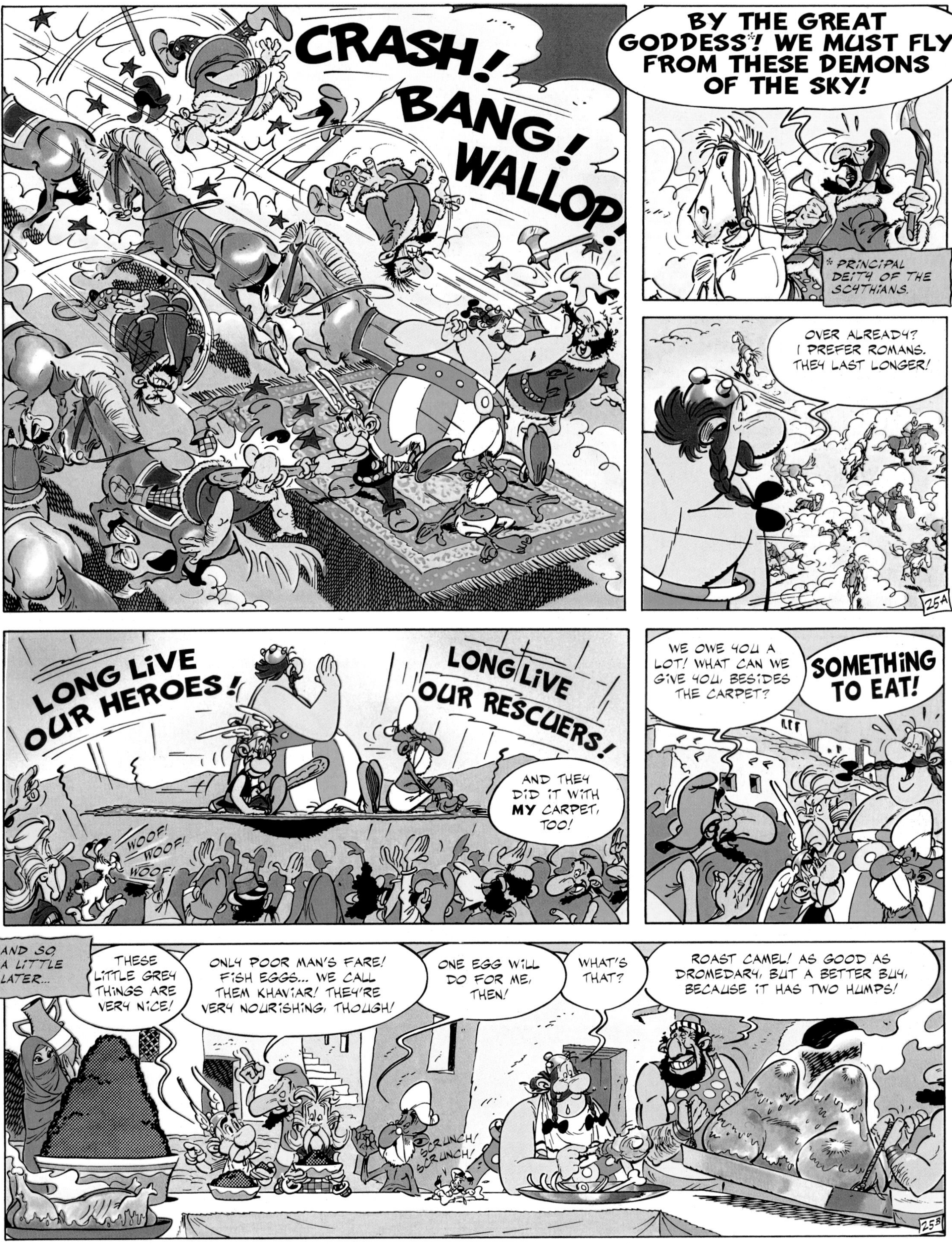
CRASH! BANG! WALLOP!
BY THE GREAT GODDESS*! WE MUST FLY FROM THESE DEMONS OF THE SKY!
* PRINCIPAL DEITY OF THE SCYTHIANS.
OVER ALREADY? I PREFER ROMANS. THEY LAST LONGER!
25A
LONG LIVE OUR HEROES!
LONG LIVE OUR RESCUERS!
AND THEY DID IT WITH MY CARPET, TOO!
WOOF! WOOF! WOOF!
WE OWE YOU A LOT! WHAT CAN WE GIVE YOU, BESIDES THE CARPET?
SOMETHING TO EAT!
AND SO A LITTLE LATER...
THESE LITTLE GREY THINGS ARE VERY NICE!
ONLY POOR MAN'S FARE! FISH EGGS... WE CALL THEM KHAVIAR! THEY'RE VERY NOURISHING, THOUGH!
ONE EGG WILL DO FOR ME, THEN!
WHAT'S THAT?
ROAST CAMEL! AS GOOD AS DROMEDARY, BUT A BETTER BUY, BECAUSE IT HAS TWO HUMPS!
SCRUNCH! SCRUNCH!
25B

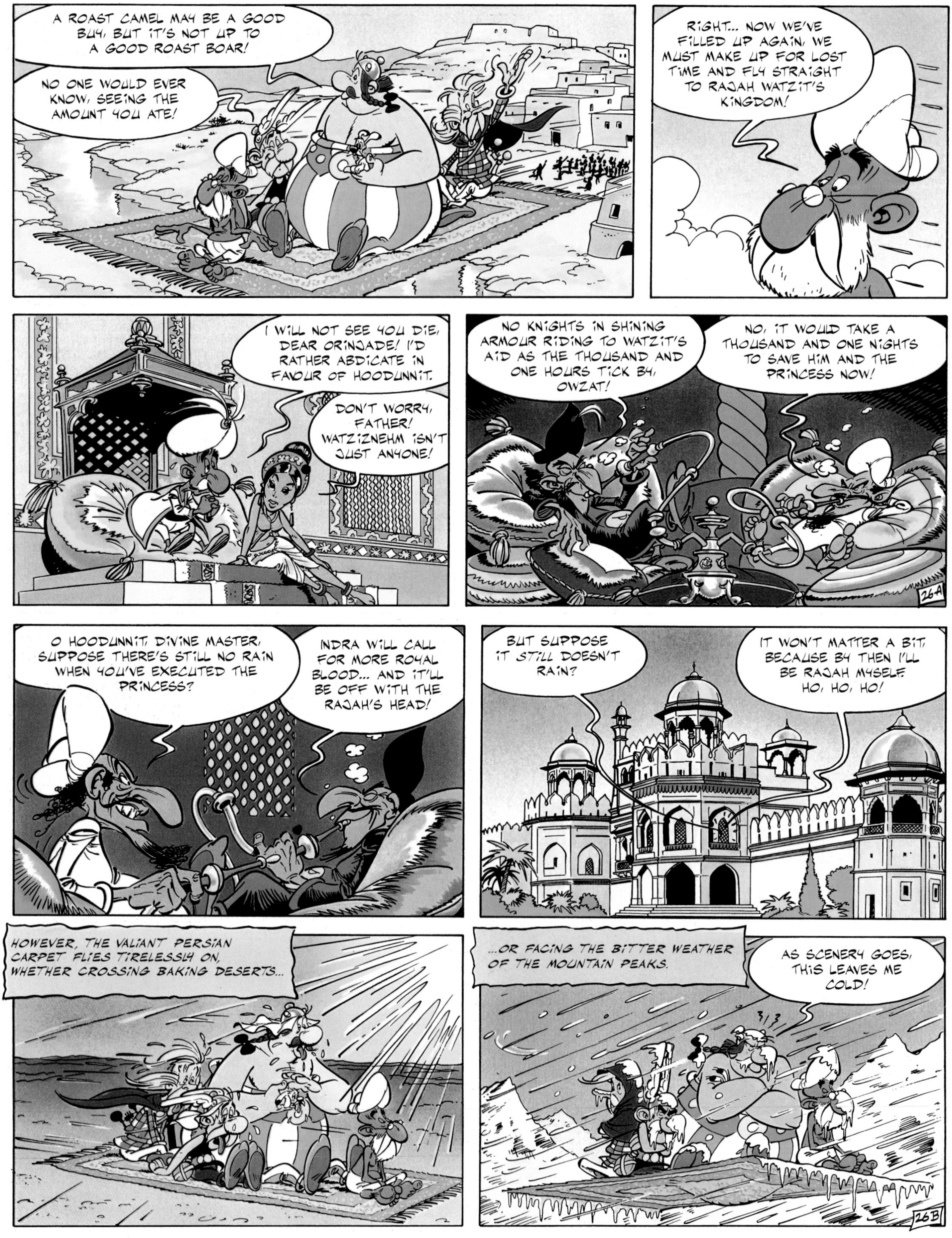

A ROAST CAMEL MAY BE A GOOD BUY, BUT IT'S NOT UP TO A GOOD ROAST BOAR!
NO ONE WOULD EVER KNOW, SEEING THE AMOUNT YOU ATE!
RIGHT... NOW WE'VE FILLED UP AGAIN, WE MUST MAKE UP FOR LOST TIME AND FLY STRAIGHT TO RAJAH WATZIT'S KINGDOM!
I WILL NOT SEE YOU DIE, DEAR ORINJADE! I'D RATHER ABDICATE IN FAVOUR OF HOODUNNIT.
DON'T WORRY, FATHER! WATZIZNEHM ISN'T JUST ANYONE!
NO KNIGHTS IN SHINING ARMOUR RIDING TO WATZIT'S AID AS THE THOUSAND AND ONE HOURS TICK BY, OWZAT!
NO, IT WOULD TAKE A THOUSAND AND ONE NIGHTS TO SAVE HIM AND THE PRINCESS NOW!
26-A
O HOODUNNIT, DIVINE MASTER, SUPPOSE THERE'S STILL NO RAIN WHEN YOU'VE EXECUTED THE PRINCESS?
INDRA WILL CALL FOR MORE ROYAL BLOOD... AND IT'LL BE OFF WITH THE RAJAH'S HEAD!
BUT SUPPOSE IT STILL DOESN'T RAIN?
IT WON'T MATTER A BIT, BECAUSE BY THEN I'LL BE RAJAH MYSELF. HO, HO, HO!
HOWEVER, THE VALIANT PERSIAN CARPET FLIES TIRELESSLY ON, WHETHER CROSSING BAKING DESERTS...
...OR FACING THE BITTER WEATHER OF THE MOUNTAIN PEAKS.
AS SCENERY GOES, THIS LEAVES ME COLD!
26B

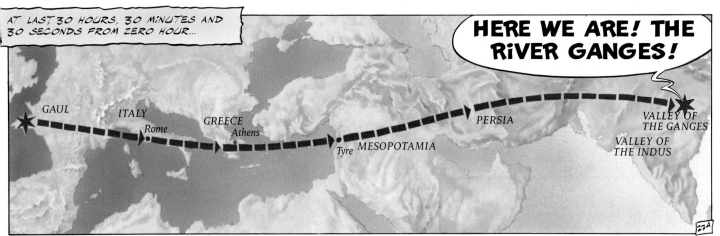

AT LAST 30 HOURS, 30 MINUTES AND 30 SECONDS FROM ZERO HOUR...

HERE WE ARE! THE RIVER GANGES!

GAUL

ITALY
Rome

GREECE
Athens

Tyre MESOPOTAMIA

PERSIA

VALLEY OF THE GANGES

VALLEY OF THE INDUS

LOOKS A BIT GUNGY, AS RIVERS GO!

WHAT ARE ALL THOSE PEOPLE DOING, SQUELCHING ABOUT IN THE MUD?

THE GANGES IS A SACRED RIVER. EVEN IN THIS DROUGHT, THE PEOPLE STILL COME HERE TO WASH, THUS PURIFYING THEIR SOULS AND BODIES. SEE?

CLEAR AS MUD! THESE INDIANS ARE CRAZY!

TAP!
TAP!
TAP!

AND HERE IS RAJAH WATZIT'S PALACE!

I SEE WATZIZNEHM'S CARPET COMING IN ... HE'S ABOUT TO BRAKE...

HE'S GOT THE GAULS ON BOARD!!! IS THIS OUR LUCKY BREAK?

CURSES!

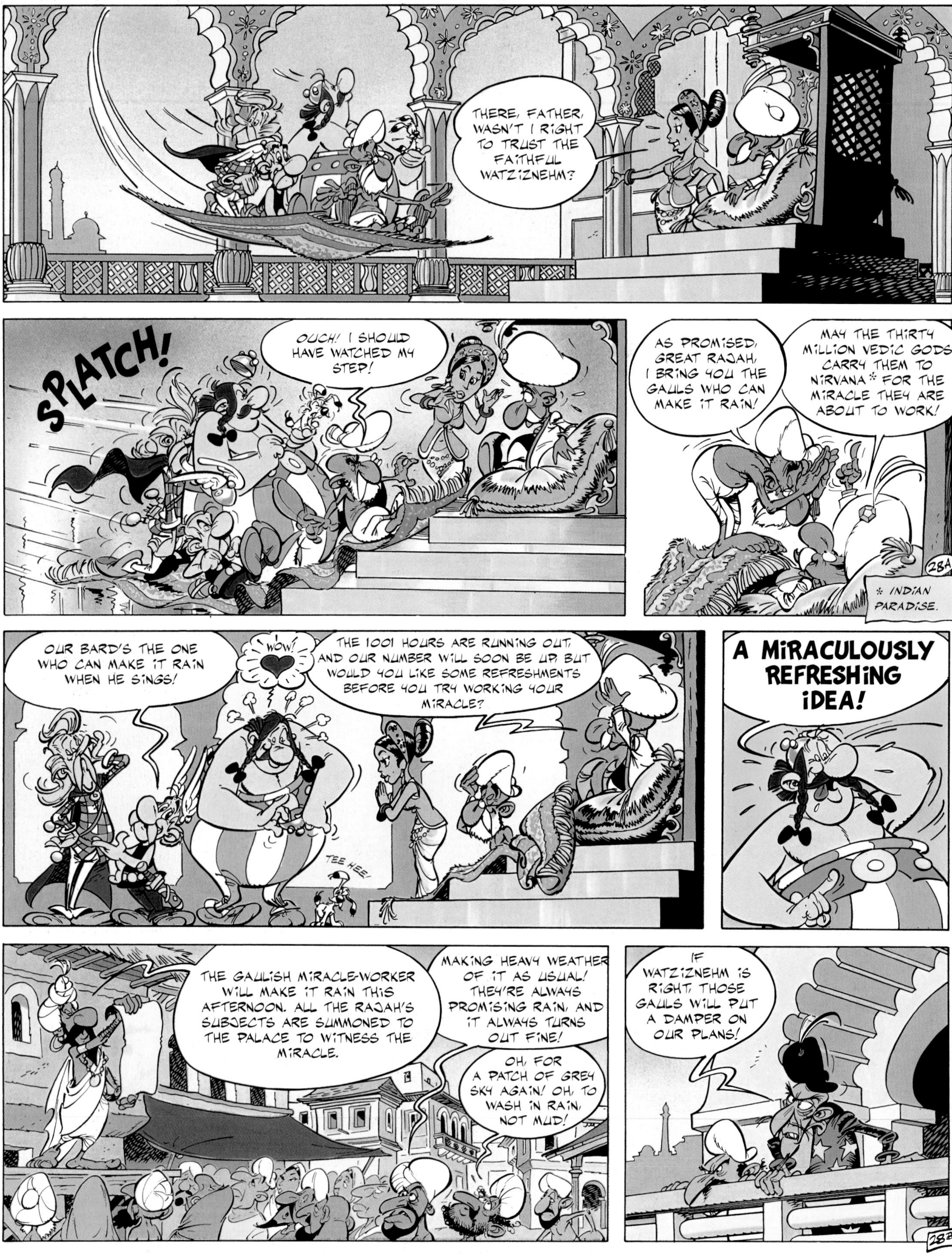

THERE, FATHER, WASN'T I RIGHT TO TRUST THE FAITHFUL WATZIZNEHM?
SPLATCH!
OUCH! I SHOULD HAVE WATCHED MY STEP!
AS PROMISED, GREAT RAJAH, I BRING YOU THE GAULS WHO CAN MAKE IT RAIN!
MAY THE THIRTY MILLION VEDIC GODS CARRY THEM TO NIRVANA* FOR THE MIRACLE THEY ARE ABOUT TO WORK!
28A
* INDIAN PARADISE.
OUR BARD'S THE ONE WHO CAN MAKE IT RAIN WHEN HE SINGS!
WOW!
THE 1001 HOURS ARE RUNNING OUT, AND OUR NUMBER WILL SOON BE UP, BUT WOULD YOU LIKE SOME REFRESHMENTS BEFORE YOU TRY WORKING YOUR MIRACLE?
TEE HEE!
A MIRACULOUSLY REFRESHING IDEA!
THE GAULISH MIRACLE-WORKER WILL MAKE IT RAIN THIS AFTERNOON. ALL THE RAJAH'S SUBJECTS ARE SUMMONED TO THE PALACE TO WITNESS THE MIRACLE.
MAKING HEAVY WEATHER OF IT AS USUAL! THEY'RE ALWAYS PROMISING RAIN, AND IT ALWAYS TURNS OUT FINE!
OH, FOR A PATCH OF GREY SKY AGAIN! OH, TO WASH IN RAIN, NOT MUD!
IF WATZIZNEHM IS RIGHT, THOSE GAULS WILL PUT A DAMPER ON OUR PLANS!
28B

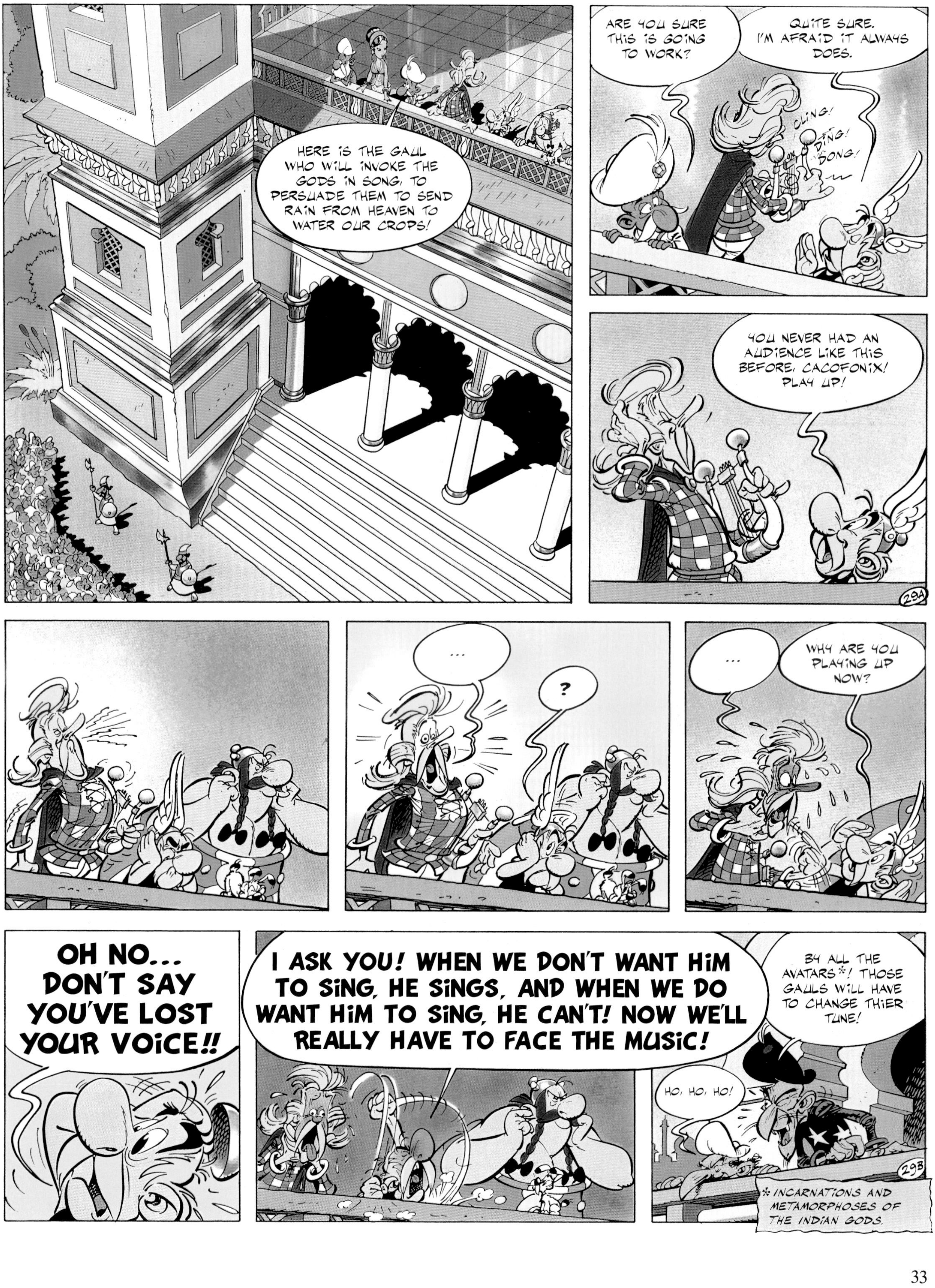
HERE IS THE GAUL WHO WILL INVOKE THE GODS IN SONG, TO PERSUADE THEM TO SEND RAIN FROM HEAVEN TO WATER OUR CROPS!
ARE YOU SURE THIS IS GOING TO WORK?
QUITE SURE. I'M AFRAID IT ALWAYS DOES.
CLING! DING! DONG!
YOU NEVER HAD AN AUDIENCE LIKE THIS BEFORE, CACOFONIX! PLAY UP!
29A
...
?
...
WHY ARE YOU PLAYING UP NOW?
OH NO... DON'T SAY YOU'VE LOST YOUR VOICE!!
I ASK YOU! WHEN WE DON'T WANT HIM TO SING, HE SINGS, AND WHEN WE DO WANT HIM TO SING, HE CAN'T! NOW WE'LL REALLY HAVE TO FACE THE MUSIC!
BY ALL THE AVATARS*! THOSE GAULS WILL HAVE TO CHANGE THIER TUNE!
HO, HO, HO!
29B
* INCARNATIONS AND METAMORPHOSES OF THE INDIAN GODS.

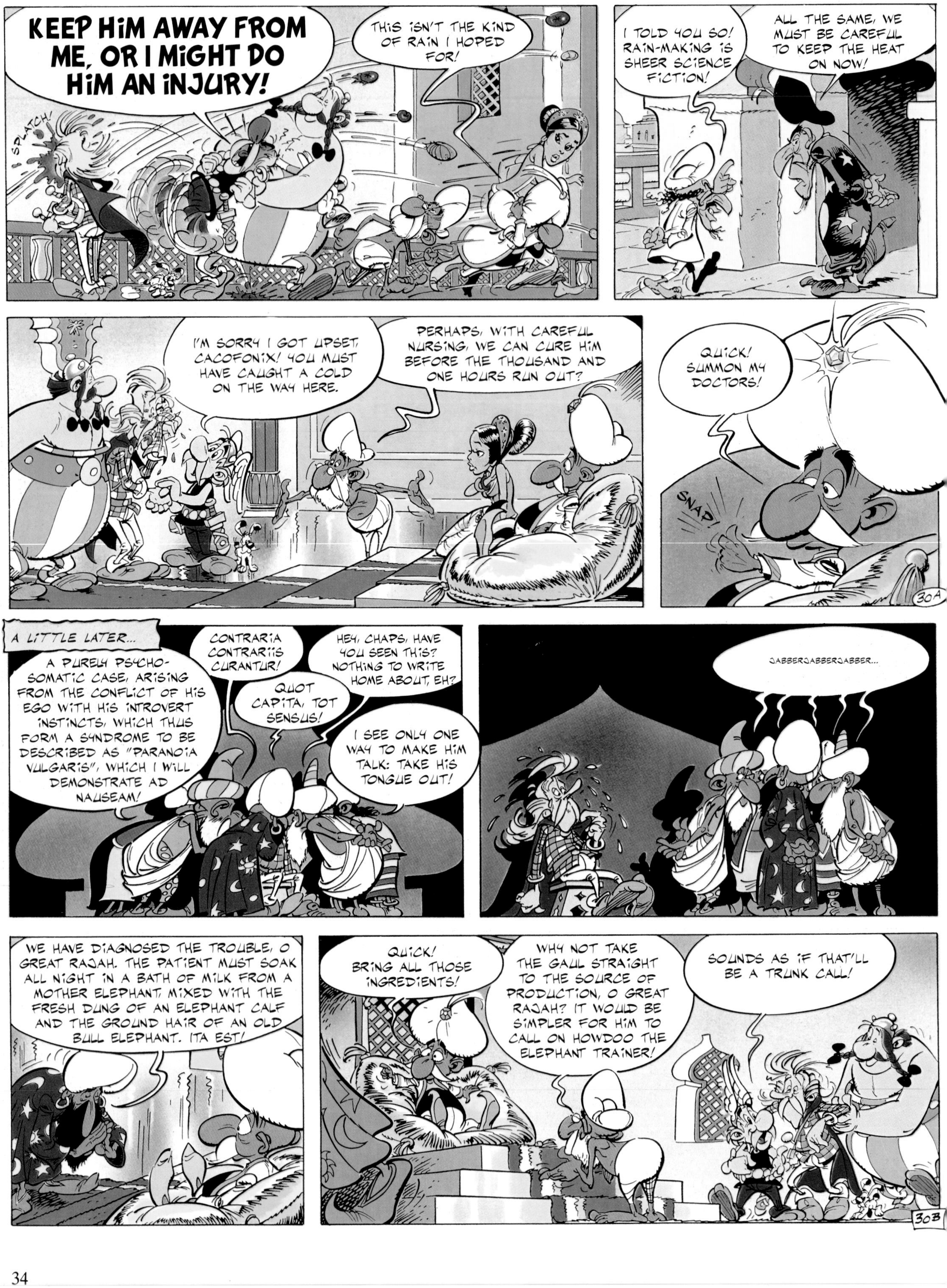
KEEP HIM AWAY FROM ME, OR I MIGHT DO HIM AN INJURY!
SPLATCH!
THIS ISN'T THE KIND OF RAIN I HOPED FOR!
I TOLD YOU SO! RAIN-MAKING IS SHEER SCIENCE FICTION!
ALL THE SAME, WE MUST BE CAREFUL TO KEEP THE HEAT ON NOW!
I'M SORRY I GOT UPSET, CACOFONIX! YOU MUST HAVE CAUGHT A COLD ON THE WAY HERE.
PERHAPS, WITH CAREFUL NURSING, WE CAN CURE HIM BEFORE THE THOUSAND AND ONE HOURS RUN OUT?
QUICK! SUMMON MY DOCTORS!
SNAP!
30A
A LITTLE LATER...
A PURELY PSYCHO-SOMATIC CASE, ARISING FROM THE CONFLICT OF HIS EGO WITH HIS INTROVERT INSTINCTS, WHICH THUS FORM A SYNDROME TO BE DESCRIBED AS "PARANOIA VULGARIS", WHICH I WILL DEMONSTRATE AD NAUSEAM!
CONTRARIA CONTRARIIS CURANTUR!
QUOT CAPITA, TOT SENSUS!
HEY, CHAPS, HAVE YOU SEEN THIS? NOTHING TO WRITE HOME ABOUT, EH?
I SEE ONLY ONE WAY TO MAKE HIM TALK: TAKE HIS TONGUE OUT!
JABBERJABBERJABBER...
WE HAVE DIAGNOSED THE TROUBLE, O GREAT RAJAH. THE PATIENT MUST SOAK ALL NIGHT IN A BATH OF MILK FROM A MOTHER ELEPHANT, MIXED WITH THE FRESH DUNG OF AN ELEPHANT CALF AND THE GROUND HAIR OF AN OLD BULL ELEPHANT. ITA EST!
QUICK! BRING ALL THOSE INGREDIENTS!
WHY NOT TAKE THE GAUL STRAIGHT TO THE SOURCE OF PRODUCTION, O GREAT RAJAH? IT WOULD BE SIMPLER FOR HIM TO CALL ON HOWDOO THE ELEPHANT TRAINER!
SOUNDS AS IF THAT'LL BE A TRUNK CALL!
30B

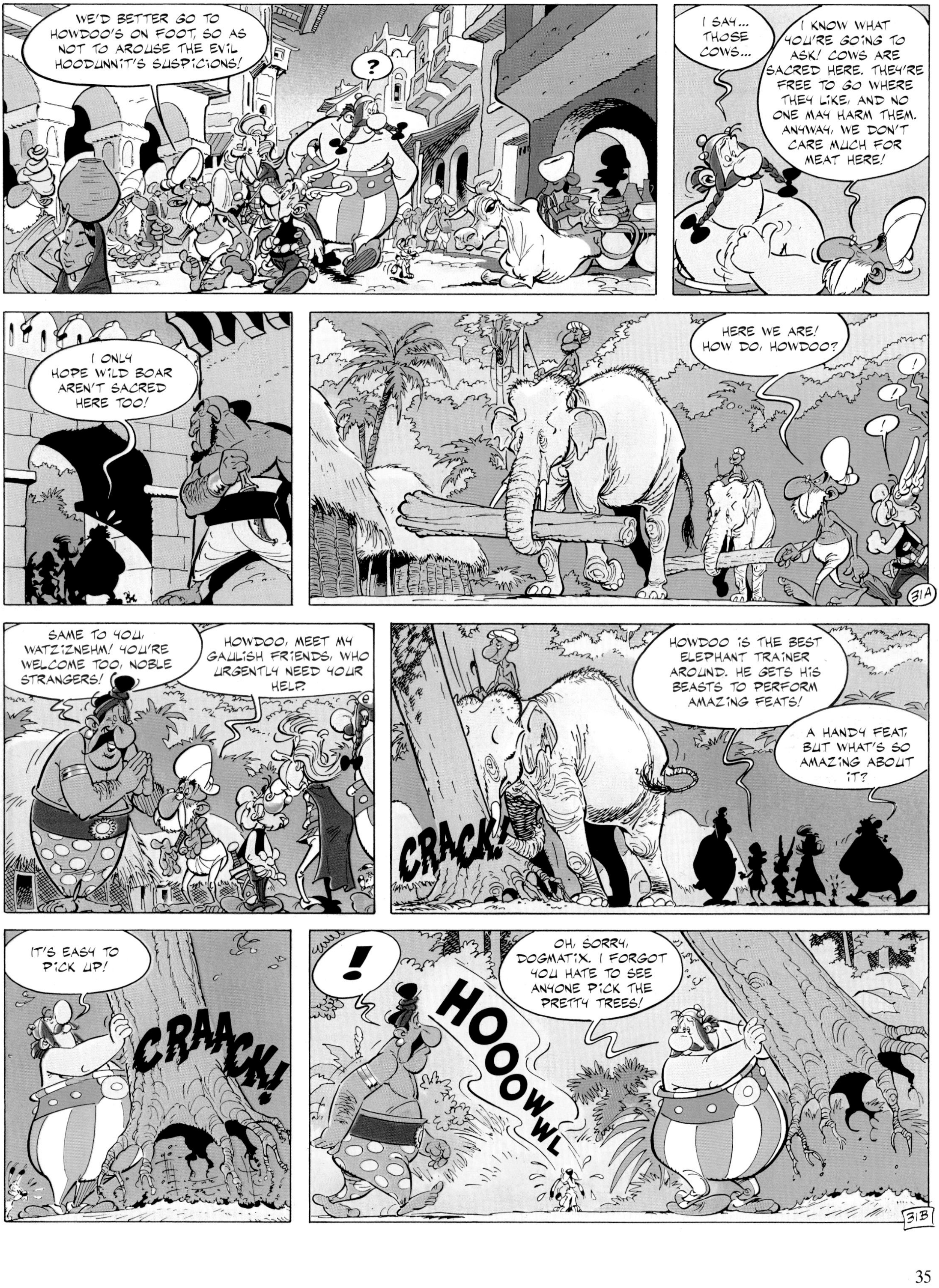

WE'D BETTER GO TO HOWDOO'S ON FOOT, SO AS NOT TO AROUSE THE EVIL HOODUNNIT'S SUSPICIONS!
?
I SAY... THOSE COWS...
I KNOW WHAT YOU'RE GOING TO ASK! COWS ARE SACRED HERE. THEY'RE FREE TO GO WHERE THEY LIKE, AND NO ONE MAY HARM THEM. ANYWAY, WE DON'T CARE MUCH FOR MEAT HERE!
I ONLY HOPE WILD BOAR AREN'T SACRED HERE TOO!
HERE WE ARE! HOW DO, HOWDOO?
!
!
!
31A
SAME TO YOU, WATZIZNEHM! YOU'RE WELCOME TOO, NOBLE STRANGERS!
HOWDOO, MEET MY GAULISH FRIENDS, WHO URGENTLY NEED YOUR HELP.
HOWDOO IS THE BEST ELEPHANT TRAINER AROUND. HE GETS HIS BEASTS TO PERFORM AMAZING FEATS!
CRACK!
A HANDY FEAT, BUT WHAT'S SO AMAZING ABOUT IT?
IT'S EASY TO PICK UP!
CRAACK!
!
HOOOWWL
OH, SORRY, DOGMATIX. I FORGOT YOU HATE TO SEE ANYONE PICK THE PRETTY TREES!
31B

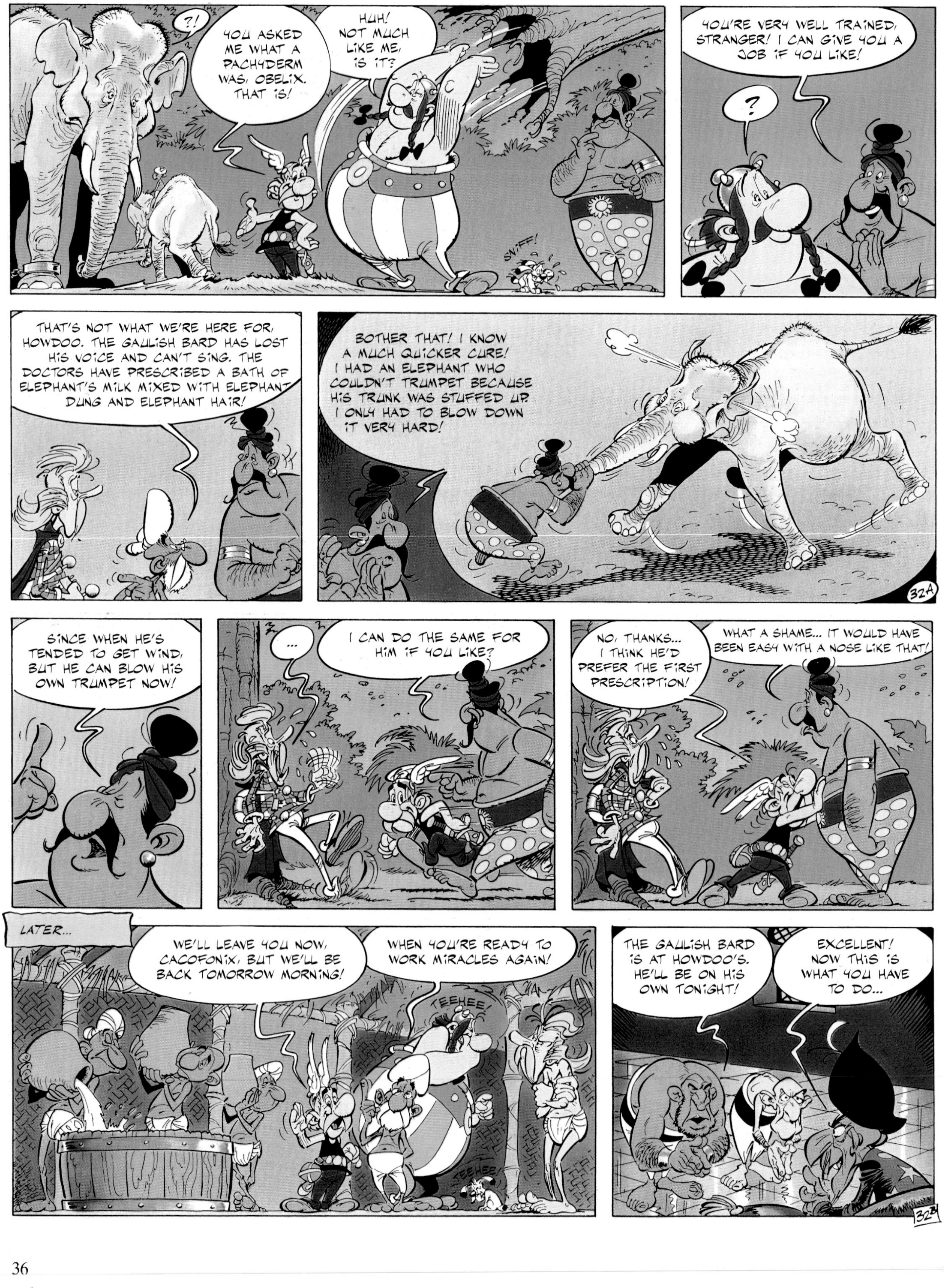
?!
YOU ASKED ME WHAT A PACHYDERM WAS, OBELIX. THAT IS!
HUH! NOT MUCH LIKE ME, IS IT?
SNIFF!
YOU'RE VERY WELL TRAINED, STRANGER! I CAN GIVE YOU A JOB IF YOU LIKE!
?
THAT'S NOT WHAT WE'RE HERE FOR, HOWDOO. THE GAULISH BARD HAS LOST HIS VOICE AND CAN'T SING. THE DOCTORS HAVE PRESCRIBED A BATH OF ELEPHANT'S MILK MIXED WITH ELEPHANT DUNG AND ELEPHANT HAIR!
BOTHER THAT! I KNOW A MUCH QUICKER CURE! I HAD AN ELEPHANT WHO COULDN'T TRUMPET BECAUSE HIS TRUNK WAS STUFFED UP. I ONLY HAD TO BLOW DOWN IT VERY HARD!
SINCE WHEN HE'S TENDED TO GET WIND, BUT HE CAN BLOW HIS OWN TRUMPET NOW!
...
I CAN DO THE SAME FOR HIM IF YOU LIKE?
NO, THANKS... I THINK HE'D PREFER THE FIRST PRESCRIPTION!
WHAT A SHAME... IT WOULD HAVE BEEN EASY WITH A NOSE LIKE THAT!
LATER...
WE'LL LEAVE YOU NOW, CACOFONIX, BUT WE'LL BE BACK TOMORROW MORNING!
WHEN YOU'RE READY TO WORK MIRACLES AGAIN!
TEEHEE!
TEEHEE
THE GAULISH BARD IS AT HOWDOO'S. HE'LL BE ON HIS OWN TONIGHT!
EXCELLENT! NOW THIS IS WHAT YOU HAVE TO DO...

WHEN NIGHT HAS FALLEN, EIGHTEEN HOURS FROM ZERO HOUR...

WHAT A PONG! IT MAKES ME GAG!

WELL, WE NEEDN'T WASTE TIME GAGGING **HIM** SINCE HE CAN'T SPEAK.

I CAN STAND MOST THINGS... THE NIGHT, THE JUNGLE, THE JUNGLE BY NIGHT, BUT THIS STINK IS TOO MUCH FOR ME!

THE SOONER WE GET THERE, THE BETTER FOR US!

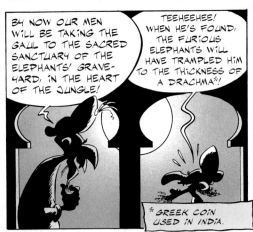

BY NOW OUR MEN WILL BE TAKING THE GAUL TO THE SACRED SANCTUARY OF THE ELEPHANTS' GRAVE-YARD, IN THE HEART OF THE JUNGLE!

TEEHEEHEE! WHEN HE'S FOUND, THE FURIOUS ELEPHANTS WILL HAVE TRAMPLED HIM TO THE THICKNESS OF A DRACHMA*!

* GREEK COIN USED IN INDIA.

NEXT MORNING, WITH TEN HOURS TO GO TO ZERO HOUR...

TIME TO GO AND GET CACOFONIX! IT'LL BE QUICKER BY CARPET!

WHAT ABOUT MY BREAKFAST?

THERE'S A TIME AND A PLACE FOR EVERYTHING!

33A

I CAN'T WAIT TO SEE IF THE CURE HAS WORKED!

I CAN'T WAIT TO KNOW WHEN IT'LL BE THE TIME AND THE PLACE FOR MY BREAKFAST. I FEEL SO FLAT WHEN MY TUMMY'S EMPTY!

AND YOUR TUMMY'S NOT THE ONLY EMPTY PART YOU!

THERE, YOU ADMIT IT YOURSELF!

THEY'RE OFF TO FETCH THE BARD! TRY TO DELAY THEM OWZAT!

THAT'S EASY... MY CARPET'S PARKED QUITE CLOSE!

NOW FOR THE SHOWDOWN, WATZiZNEHM!

33B

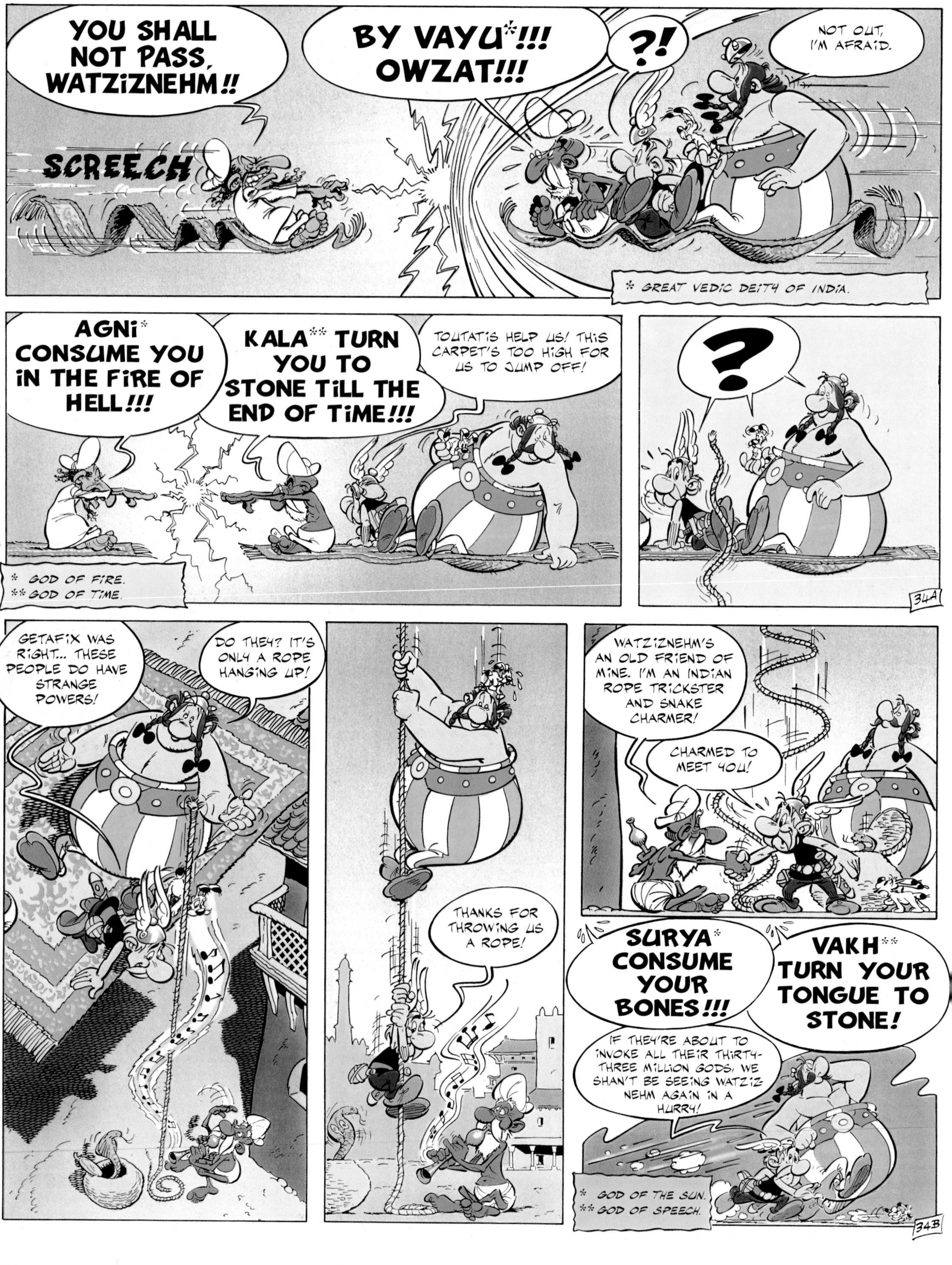
YOU SHALL NOT PASS, WATZiZNEHM!!
SCREECH
BY VAYU*!!! OWZAT!!!
?!
NOT OUT, I'M AFRAID.
* GREAT VEDIC DEITY OF INDIA.
AGNi* CONSUME YOU iN THE FiRE OF HELL!!!
KALA** TURN YOU TO STONE TiLL THE END OF TiME!!!
TOUTATiS HELP US! THiS CARPET'S TOO HIGH FOR US TO JUMP OFF!
* GOD OF FIRE.
** GOD OF TIME.
?
34A
GETAFiX WAS RiGHT... THESE PEOPLE DO HAVE STRANGE POWERS!
DO THEY? IT'S ONLY A ROPE HANGiNG UP!
THANKS FOR THROWiNG US A ROPE!
WATZiZNEHM'S AN OLD FRiEND OF MiNE. I'M AN INDIAN ROPE TRiCKSTER AND SNAKE CHARMER!
CHARMED TO MEET YOU!
SURYA* CONSUME YOUR BONES!!!
VAKH** TURN YOUR TONGUE TO STONE!
IF THEY'RE ABOUT TO iNVOKE ALL THEiR THiRTY-THREE MiLLiON GODS, WE SHAN'T BE SEEiNG WATZiZNEHM AGAiN iN A HURRY!
* GOD OF THE SUN.
** GOD OF SPEECH.
34B

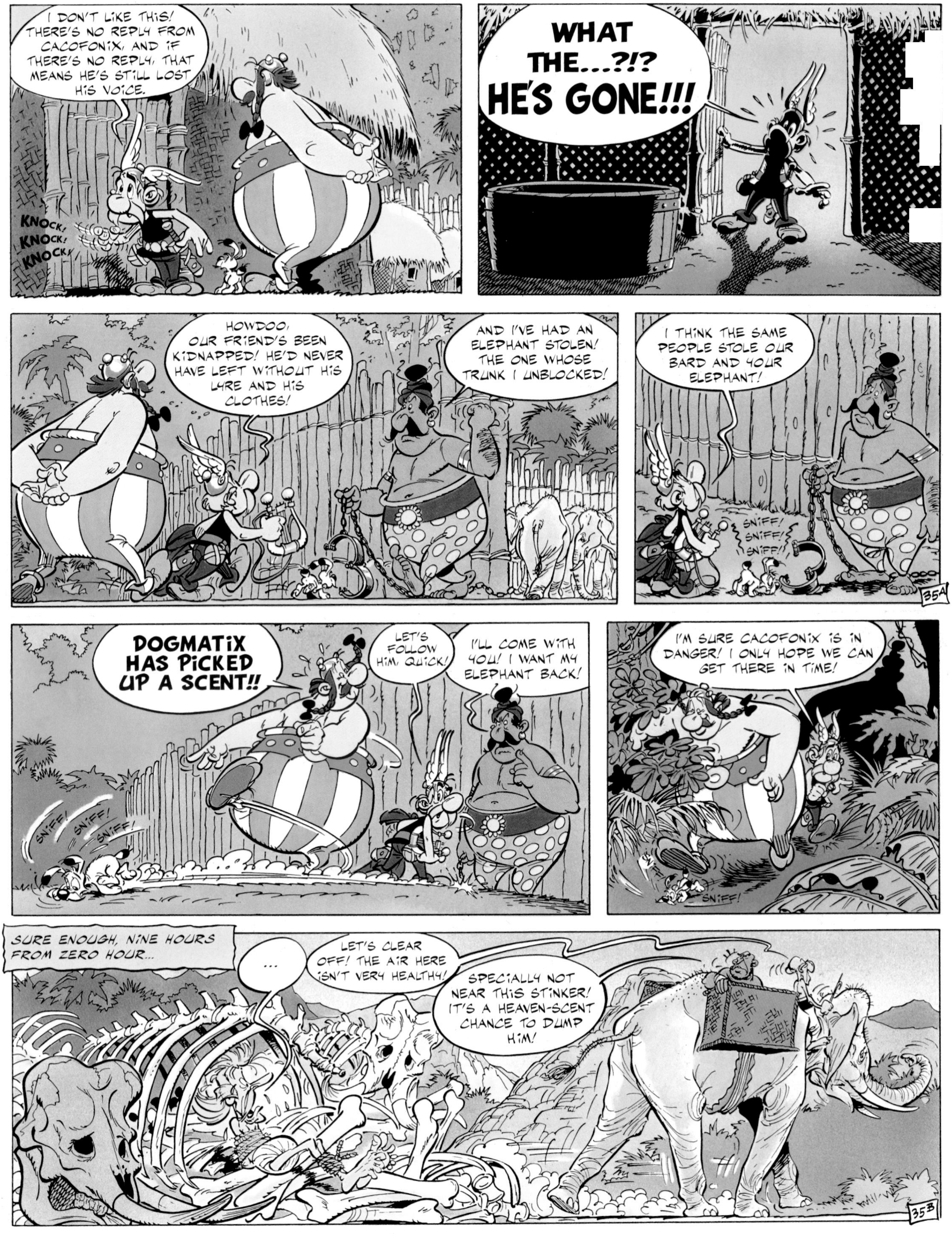
I DON'T LIKE THIS! THERE'S NO REPLY FROM CACOFONIX, AND IF THERE'S NO REPLY, THAT MEANS HE'S STILL LOST HIS VOICE.
KNOCK! KNOCK! KNOCK!
WHAT THE...?!? HE'S GONE!!!
HOWDOO, OUR FRIEND'S BEEN KIDNAPPED! HE'D NEVER HAVE LEFT WITHOUT HIS LYRE AND HIS CLOTHES!
AND I'VE HAD AN ELEPHANT STOLEN! THE ONE WHOSE TRUNK I UNBLOCKED!
I THINK THE SAME PEOPLE STOLE OUR BARD AND YOUR ELEPHANT!
SNIFF! SNIFF! SNIFF!
35A
DOGMATIX HAS PICKED UP A SCENT!!
LET'S FOLLOW HIM, QUICK!
I'LL COME WITH YOU! I WANT MY ELEPHANT BACK!
SNIFF! SNIFF! SNIFF!
I'M SURE CACOFONIX IS IN DANGER! I ONLY HOPE WE CAN GET THERE IN TIME!
SNIFF!
SURE ENOUGH, NINE HOURS FROM ZERO HOUR...
...
LET'S CLEAR OFF! THE AIR HERE ISN'T VERY HEALTHY!
SPECIALLY NOT NEAR THIS STINKER! IT'S A HEAVEN-SCENT CHANCE TO DUMP HIM!
35B

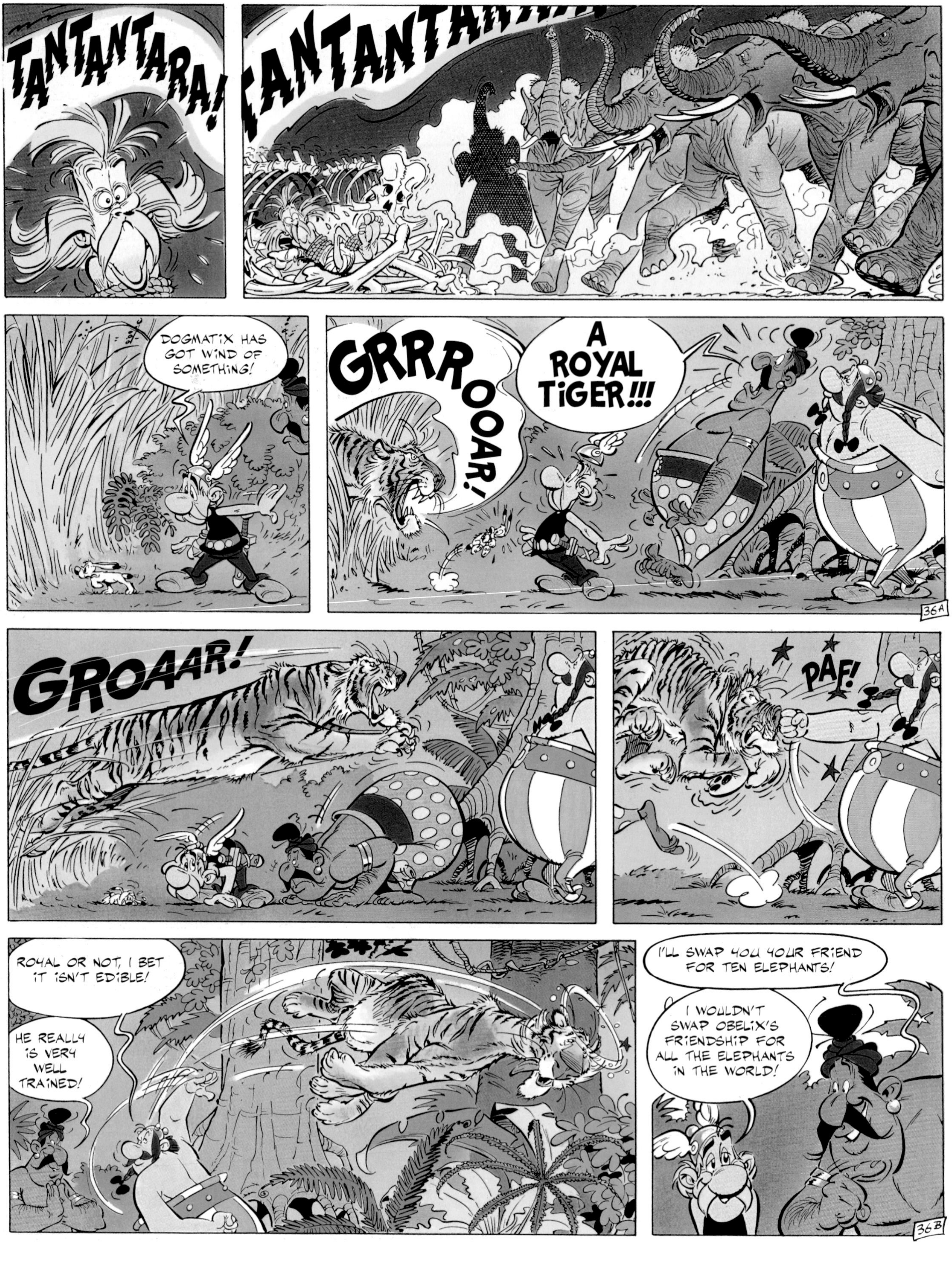

TANTANTARA!
DOGMATIX HAS GOT WIND OF SOMETHING!
GRRROOAR!
A ROYAL TIGER!!!
36A
GROAAR!
PAF!
ROYAL OR NOT, I BET IT ISN'T EDIBLE!
HE REALLY IS VERY WELL TRAINED!
I'LL SWAP YOU YOUR FRIEND FOR TEN ELEPHANTS!
I WOULDN'T SWAP OBELIX'S FRIENDSHIP FOR ALL THE ELEPHANTS IN THE WORLD!
36B

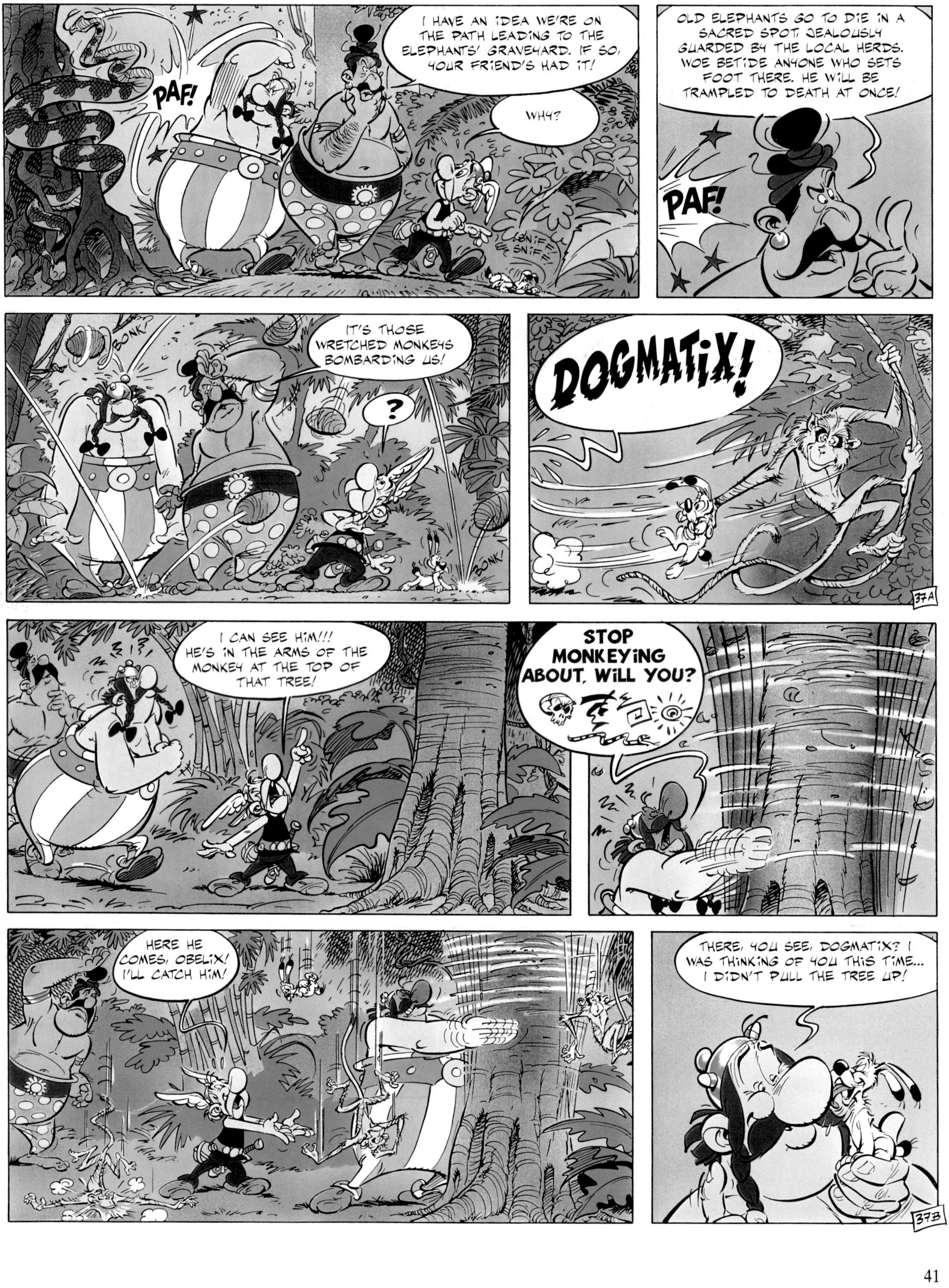
PAF!
I HAVE AN IDEA WE'RE ON THE PATH LEADING TO THE ELEPHANTS' GRAVEYARD. IF SO, YOUR FRIEND'S HAD IT!
WHY?
SNIFF SNIFF
OLD ELEPHANTS GO TO DIE IN A SACRED SPOT, JEALOUSLY GUARDED BY THE LOCAL HERDS. WOE BETIDE ANYONE WHO SETS FOOT THERE. HE WILL BE TRAMPLED TO DEATH AT ONCE!
PAF!
BONK!
IT'S THOSE WRETCHED MONKEYS BOMBARDING US!
?
BONK!
DOGMATIX!
37A
I CAN SEE HIM!!! HE'S IN THE ARMS OF THE MONKEY AT THE TOP OF THAT TREE!
STOP MONKEYING ABOUT, WILL YOU?
HERE HE COMES, OBELIX! I'LL CATCH HIM!
THERE, YOU SEE, DOGMATIX? I WAS THINKING OF YOU THIS TIME... I DIDN'T PULL THE TREE UP!
37B

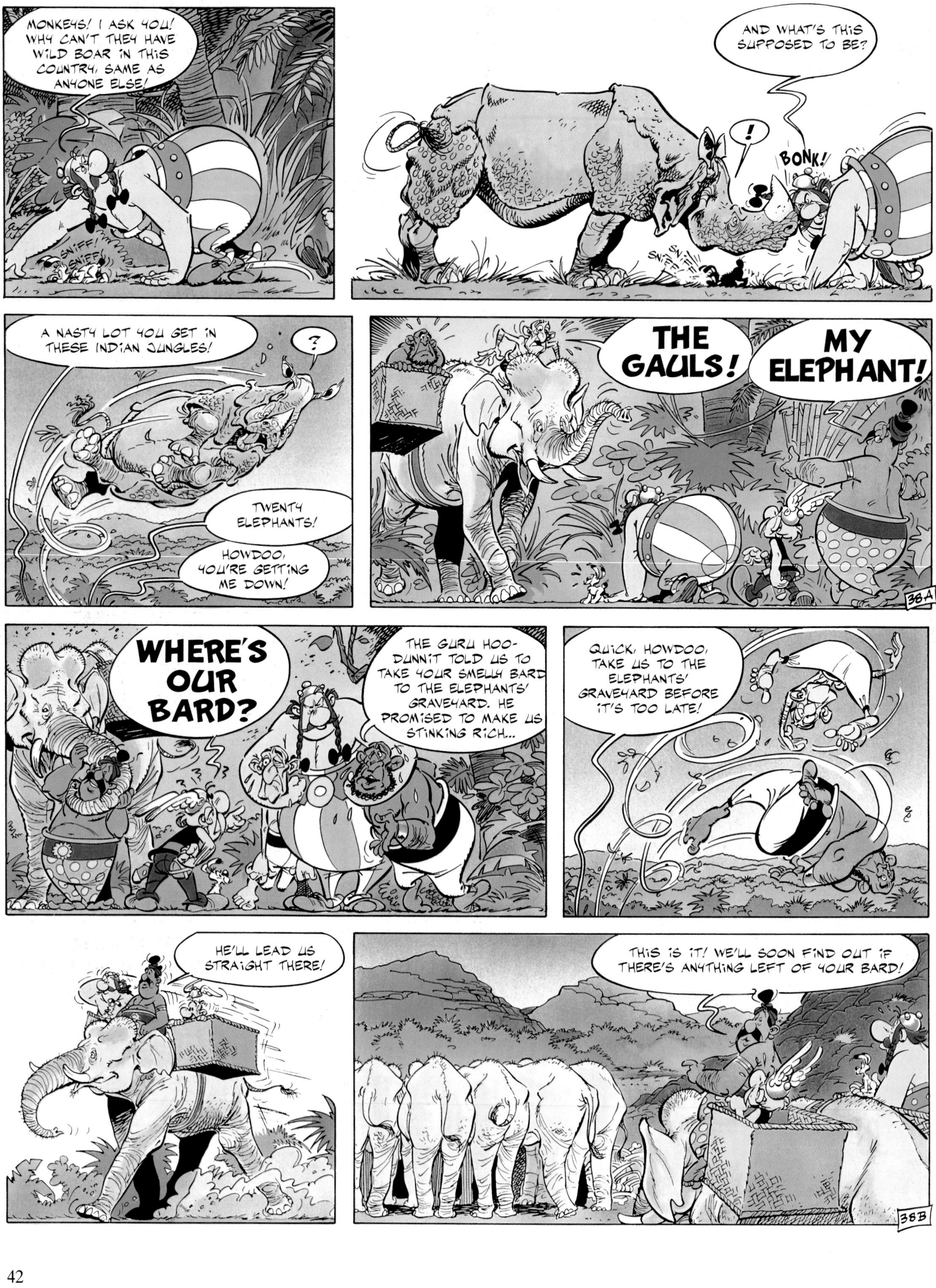

MONKEYS! I ASK YOU! WHY CAN'T THEY HAVE WILD BOAR IN THIS COUNTRY, SAME AS ANYONE ELSE!
SNIFF! SNIFF!
AND WHAT'S THIS SUPPOSED TO BE?
!
BONK!
SNIFF SNIFF
A NASTY LOT YOU GET IN THESE INDIAN JUNGLES!
?
TWENTY ELEPHANTS!
HOWDOO, YOU'RE GETTING ME DOWN!
THE GAULS!
MY ELEPHANT!
38A
WHERE'S OUR BARD?
THE GURU HOO-DUNNIT TOLD US TO TAKE YOUR SMELLY BARD TO THE ELEPHANTS' GRAVEYARD. HE PROMISED TO MAKE US STINKING RICH...
QUICK, HOWDOO, TAKE US TO THE ELEPHANTS' GRAVEYARD BEFORE IT'S TOO LATE!
HE'LL LEAD US STRAIGHT THERE!
THIS IS IT! WE'LL SOON FIND OUT IF THERE'S ANYTHING LEFT OF YOUR BARD!
38B

TANTAN AAARAT

TRUMPETING NICELY NOW, ISN'T HE?

THE ELEPHANTS ARE MOVING ASIDE!

THANK TOUTATIS HE'S SAFE AND SOUND!!!

THANKS TO THE SMELL CLINGING TO HIM, THE ELEPHANTS THOUGHT HE WAS ONE OF THEM! WHAT LUCK FOR HIM!

I KNEW I HAD NOTHING IN COMMON WITH THOSE PACHYDERMS!

YOU'VE STILL LOST YOUR VOICE, BUT YOU'RE ALIVE, THAT'S THE MAIN THING!

TANTANTARAAAA!

BUT WE ARE NOW ONLY TWO HOURS FROM ZERO HOUR, AND PREPARATIONS FOR THE SACRIFICE ARE ALREADY UNDER WAY.

I SHALL DISPOSE OF THE DAUGHTER FIRST, THEN THE FATHER, AND THEN, LIKE MY COUSIN IZNOGOUD, I SHALL BE RAJAH INSTEAD OF THE RAJAH!

WHAT CAN THE GAULS BE DOING? WHERE IS WATZIZNEHM?

WATZIZNEHM IS STILL BUSY WITH HIS SUMMIT MEETING. WHICH OF THE TWO FAKIRS WILL WIN? WATZIZNEHM? OWZAT? IT'S ALL STILL IN THE AIR...

SKAMBHA* BRING THE SKY DOWN ON YOUR HEAD!!

PUSHAN** TURN YOU INTO AN OLD GOAT!

* COSMIC PILLAR GOD HOLDING UP THE SKY.   ** GOD OF DOMESTIC ANIMALS.

43

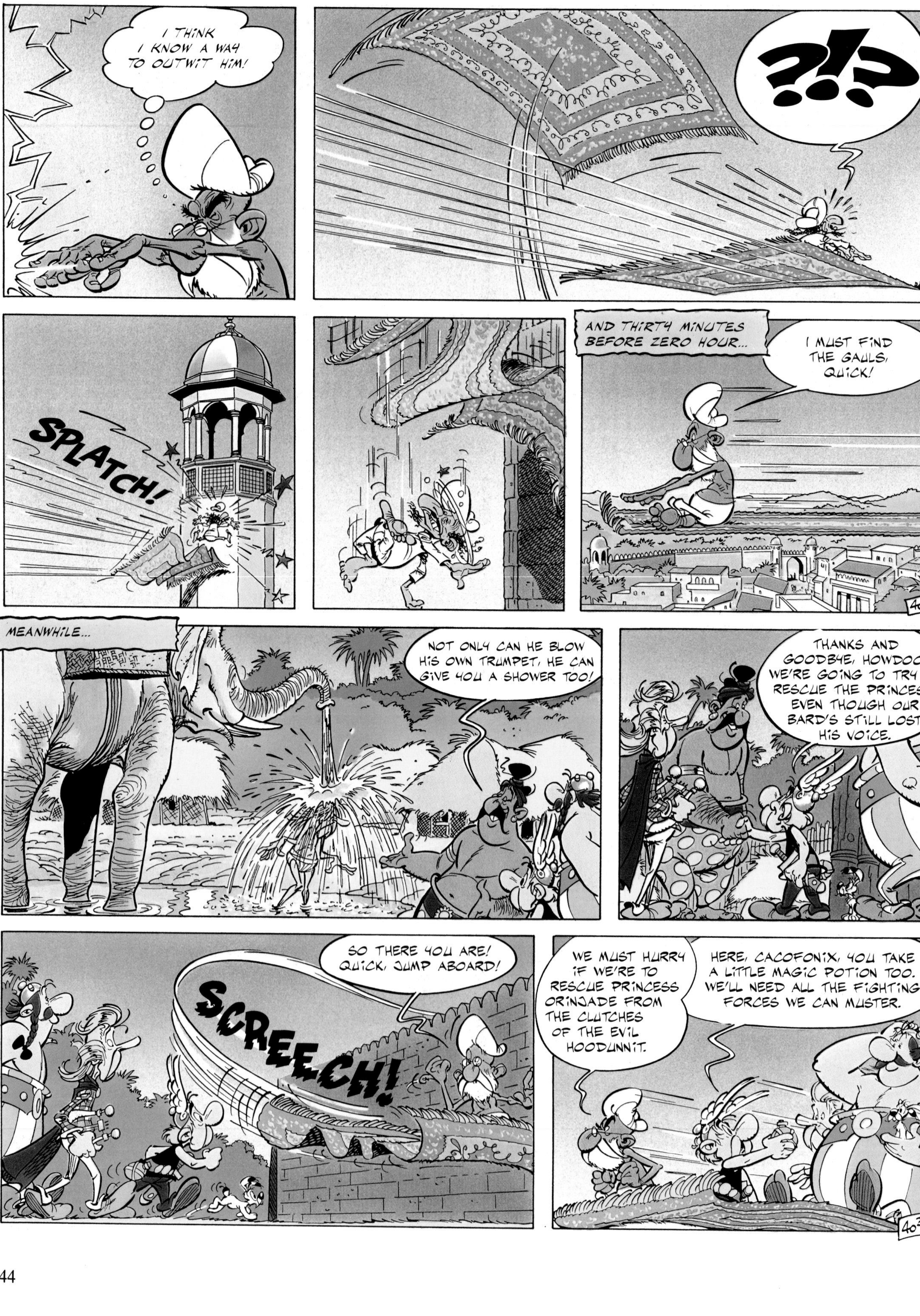
I THINK I KNOW A WAY TO OUTWIT HIM!
?!?
SPLATCH!
AND THIRTY MINUTES BEFORE ZERO HOUR...
I MUST FIND THE GAULS, QUICK!
40A
MEANWHILE...
NOT ONLY CAN HE BLOW HIS OWN TRUMPET, HE CAN GIVE YOU A SHOWER TOO!
THANKS AND GOODBYE, HOWDOO. WE'RE GOING TO TRY TO RESCUE THE PRINCESS, EVEN THOUGH OUR BARD'S STILL LOST HIS VOICE.
SO THERE YOU ARE! QUICK, JUMP ABOARD!
SCREECH!
WE MUST HURRY IF WE'RE TO RESCUE PRINCESS ORINJADE FROM THE CLUTCHES OF THE EVIL HOODUNNIT.
HERE, CACOFONIX, YOU TAKE A LITTLE MAGIC POTION TOO. WE'LL NEED ALL THE FIGHTING FORCES WE CAN MUSTER.
40B

AT FIVE MINUTES TO ZERO HOUR...

BETTER RESIGN YOURSELF, PRINCESS! STILL NO RAIN! YOUR LAST HOUR HAS COME!

MAY VISHNU* STRANGLE YOU, EVIL GURU!

* GOD WITH MANY ARMS.

MAY MY SACRIFICE PERSUADE HEAVEN TO SHOWER ITS BLESSINGS ON YOU ONCE AGAIN! IF IT DOES NOT, BEWARE OF THOSE SERPENTS WHO ARE TRICKING YOU FOR THEIR OWN EVIL ENDS!

41A

LONG LIVE OUR PRINCESS WHO IS ABOUT TO DIE FOR US!!!

POOR SILLY IDIOTS!

FIVE... FOUR... THREE...

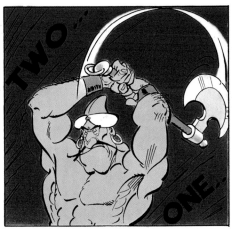

TWO... ONE...

ZERO!

TCHAC!

41B

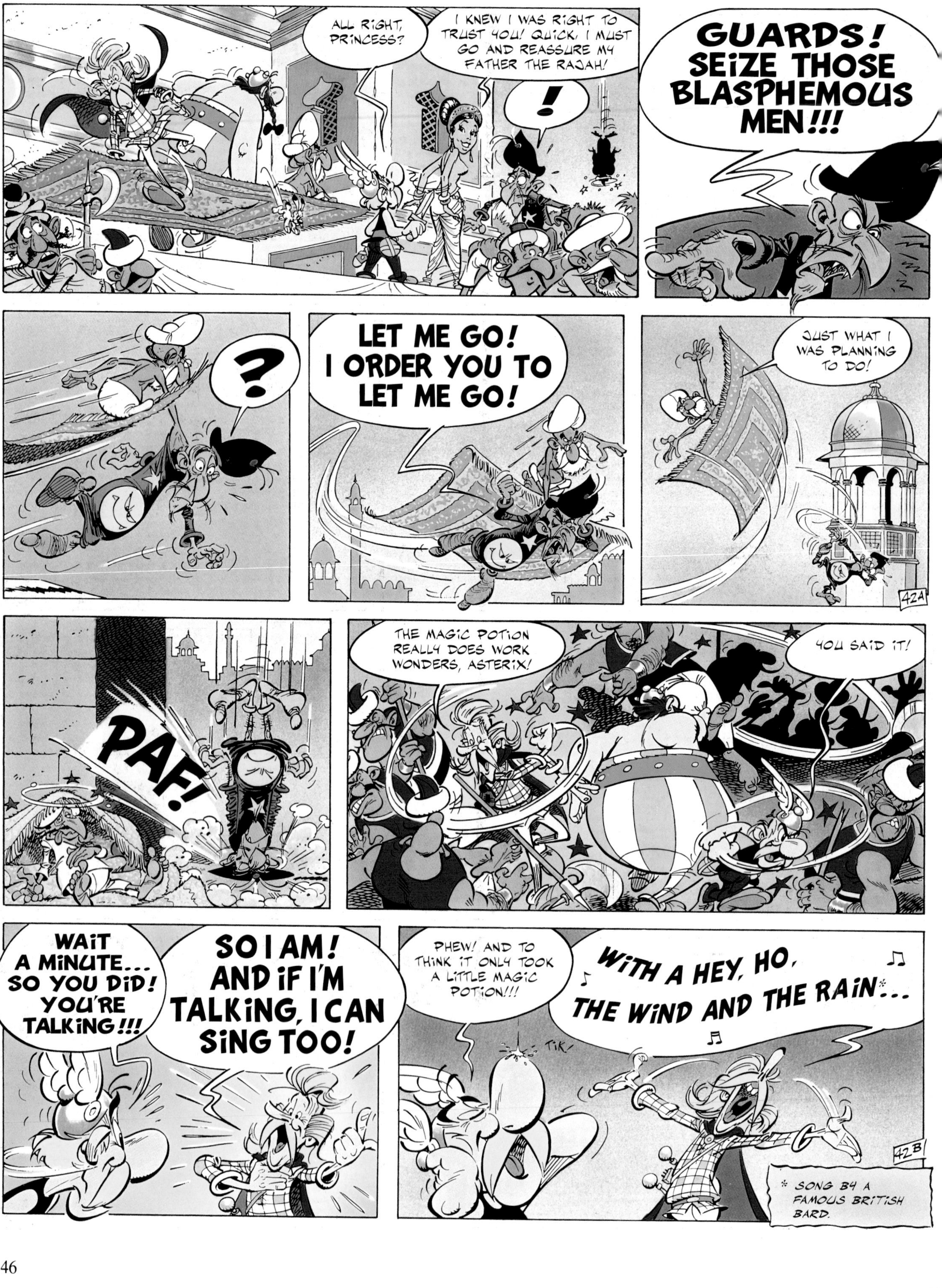
ALL RIGHT, PRINCESS?
I KNEW I WAS RIGHT TO TRUST YOU! QUICK, I MUST GO AND REASSURE MY FATHER THE RAJAH!
!
GUARDS! SEIZE THOSE BLASPHEMOUS MEN!!!
?
LET ME GO! I ORDER YOU TO LET ME GO!
JUST WHAT I WAS PLANNING TO DO!
42A
PAF!
THE MAGIC POTION REALLY DOES WORK WONDERS, ASTERIX!
YOU SAID IT!
WAIT A MINUTE... SO YOU DID! YOU'RE TALKING!!!
SO I AM! AND IF I'M TALKING, I CAN SING TOO!
PHEW! AND TO THINK IT ONLY TOOK A LITTLE MAGIC POTION!!!
TIK!
WITH A HEY, HO, THE WIND AND THE RAIN*...
42B
* SONG BY A FAMOUS BRITISH BARD.

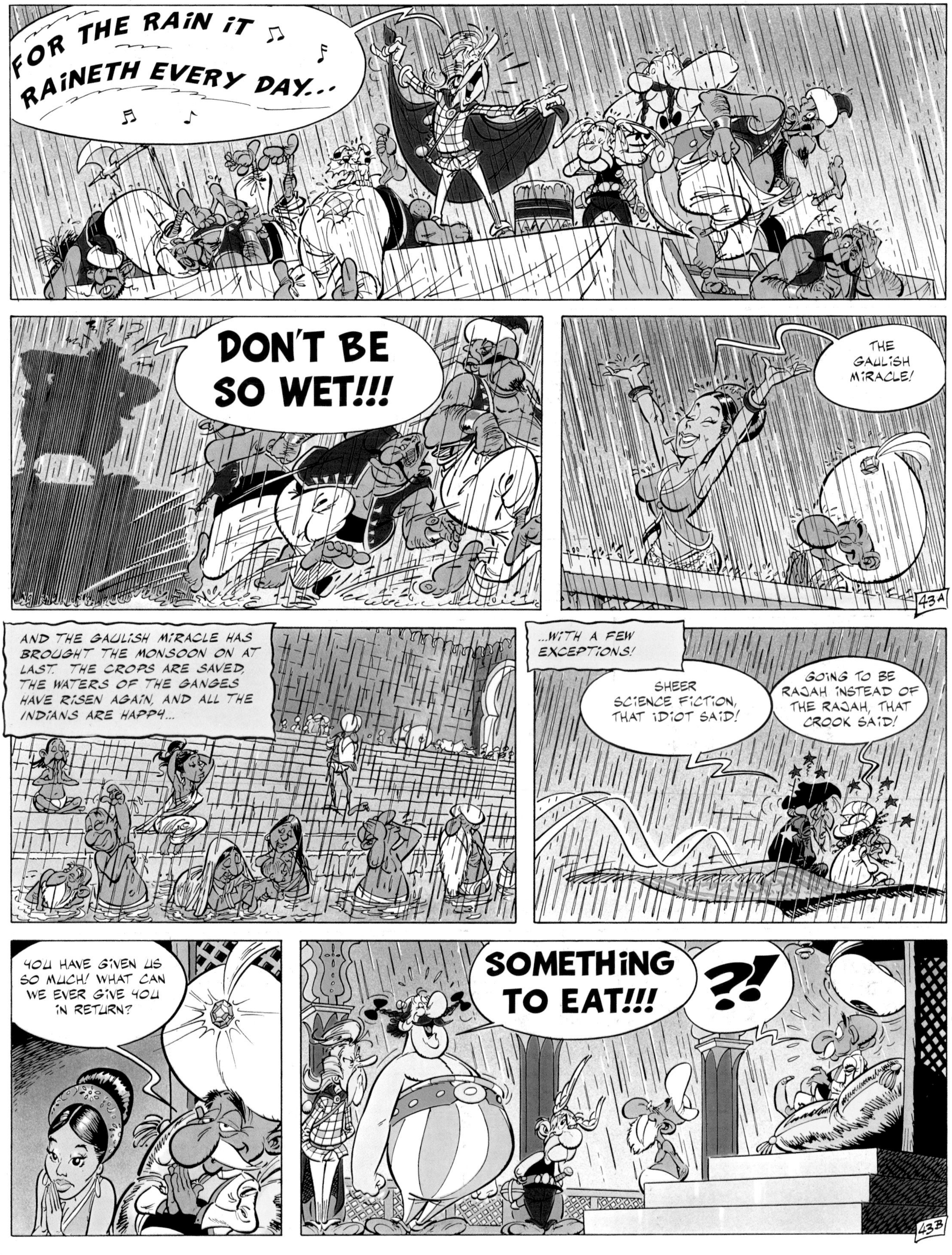
FOR THE RAIN IT RAINETH EVERY DAY...
DON'T BE SO WET!!!
THE GAULISH MIRACLE!
43A
AND THE GAULISH MIRACLE HAS BROUGHT THE MONSOON ON AT LAST. THE CROPS ARE SAVED, THE WATERS OF THE GANGES HAVE RISEN AGAIN, AND ALL THE INDIANS ARE HAPPY...
...WITH A FEW EXCEPTIONS!
SHEER SCIENCE FICTION, THAT IDIOT SAID!
GOING TO BE RAJAH INSTEAD OF THE RAJAH, THAT CROOK SAID!
YOU HAVE GIVEN US SO MUCH! WHAT CAN WE EVER GIVE YOU IN RETURN?
SOMETHING TO EAT!!!
?!
43B

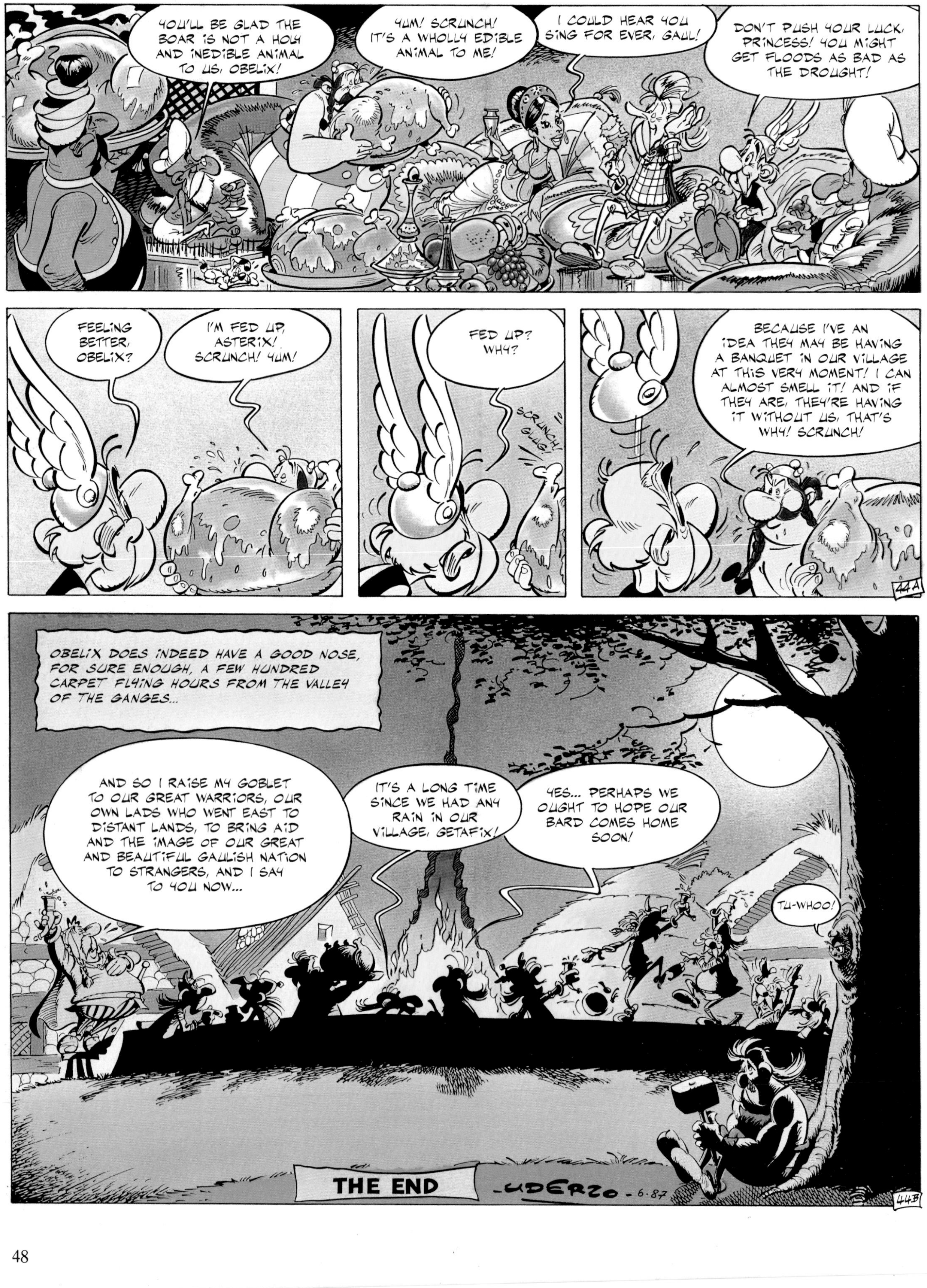
YOU'LL BE GLAD THE BOAR IS NOT A HOLY AND INEDIBLE ANIMAL TO US, OBELIX!
YUM! SCRUNCH! IT'S A WHOLLY EDIBLE ANIMAL TO ME!
I COULD HEAR YOU SING FOR EVER, GAUL!
DON'T PUSH YOUR LUCK, PRINCESS! YOU MIGHT GET FLOODS AS BAD AS THE DROUGHT!
FEELING BETTER, OBELIX?
I'M FED UP, ASTERIX! SCRUNCH! YUM!
FED UP? WHY?
SCRUNCH! GLUG!
BECAUSE I'VE AN IDEA THEY MAY BE HAVING A BANQUET IN OUR VILLAGE AT THIS VERY MOMENT! I CAN ALMOST SMELL IT! AND IF THEY ARE, THEY'RE HAVING IT WITHOUT US, THAT'S WHY! SCRUNCH!
44A
OBELIX DOES INDEED HAVE A GOOD NOSE, FOR SURE ENOUGH, A FEW HUNDRED CARPET FLYING HOURS FROM THE VALLEY OF THE GANGES...
AND SO I RAISE MY GOBLET TO OUR GREAT WARRIORS, OUR OWN LADS WHO WENT EAST TO DISTANT LANDS, TO BRING AID AND THE IMAGE OF OUR GREAT AND BEAUTIFUL GAULISH NATION TO STRANGERS, AND I SAY TO YOU NOW...
IT'S A LONG TIME SINCE WE HAD ANY RAIN IN OUR VILLAGE, GETAFIX!
YES... PERHAPS WE OUGHT TO HOPE OUR BARD COMES HOME SOON!
TU-WHOO!
THE END
UDERZO - 6.87
44B

Asterix titles available now

Coming soon

Original title: *Astérix chez Rahãzade*

Exclusive Licensee: Orion Publishing Group
Translators: Anthea Bell and Derek Hockridge
Typography: Bryony Newhouse

This revised edition first published in 2002 by Orion Books Ltd
Orion House, 5 Upper St Martin's Lane London WC2H 9EA

Printed in Italy

http://gb.asterix.com
www.orionbooks.co.uk

A CIP catalogue record for this book is available from the British Library

ISBN 0 75284715 5 (cased)
ISBN 0 75284 776 7 (paperback)

Distributed in the United States of America by Sterling Publishing Co., Inc
387 Park Avenue South, New York, NY 10016-8810

GOSCINNY AND UDERZO

PRESENT

An Asterix Adventure

ASTERIX
AND THE
MAGIC CARPET

Written and Illustrated by ALBERT UDERZO

Translated by ANTHEA BELL *and* DEREK HOCKRIDGE